RIPTIDE!

In an instant, Carole was completely submerged in the surf. This time, instead of propelling her upward and toward the shore, it pulled her down, tugging fiercely at her feet, dragging her down to the sandy bottom.

Carole had never felt a force like this. There was no fighting it. It was mightier than a team of horses, stronger than anything she'd ever known. Her hair swarmed around her, tugged every which way by the water. Her body scraped the bottom, and where the sand had once seemed silky, it now abraded her skin. And her lungs screamed for air . . . .

THE SADDLE CLUB

BEACH RIDE

BONNIE BRYANT

A BANTAM SKYLARK BOOK®
NEW YORK · TORONTO · LONDON · SYDNEY · AUCKLAND

RL 5, 009–012

BEACH RIDE
A Bantam Skylark Book / February 1993

Skylark Books is a registered trademark of Bantam Books,
a division of Bantam Doubleday Dell Publishing Group, Inc.
Registered in U.S. Patent and Trademark Office and elsewhere.

"The Saddle Club" is a trademark of Bonnie Bryant Hiller.
The Saddle Club design/logo, which consists of an inverted
U-shaped design, a riding crop, and a riding hat is a
trademark of Bantam Books.

ISBN 0-553-48073-1

Published simultaneously in the United States and Canada

Bantam Books are published by Bantam Books, a division of Bantam Doubleday Dell Publishing Group, Inc. Its trademark, consist-
ing of the words "Bantam Books" and the portrayal of a rooster, is
Registered in U.S. Patent and Trademark Office and in other coun-
tries. Marca Registrada. Bantam Books, 666 Fifth Avenue, New
York, New York 10103.

PRINTED IN THE UNITED STATES OF AMERICA

CWO   0 9 8 7 6 5 4 3 2 1

For Emmons B. Hiller

"GIRLS, I WANT to introduce you to a new rider," Max Regnery said. "This is Alice Jackson. Alice, I'd like you to meet Lisa Atwood, Stevie Lake, and Carole Hanson."

The three members of The Saddle Club had been trying to untangle some tack. It took them a few seconds to disengage themselves from the mass of leathers, but the three girls smiled a welcome to the newcomer. She nodded shyly in return. Alice was a girl about their own age. She was tall and slender. She had long dark hair that she wore in a neat braid. She carried a riding hat under one arm and her riding clothes had a nice used look. With one glance, Stevie,

Lisa, and Carole figured out that Alice already knew a lot about riding. That made her their kind of rider.

"Class starts in fifteen minutes," Max said, looking at his watch in his not-too-subtle manner. He hated it when his students were late to class. "Can one of you help Alice tack up Comanche for the flat class?"

"I'll do it," Lisa volunteered. "I'm riding Barq today, and he's already got his saddle on." She glanced at her friends and felt a twinge of guilt about leaving them with the tangle of bridles.

"Go ahead," Stevie assured her. "Four hands in this mess are enough. We'll see you in class."

Carole nodded to show her agreement. Then, as if to prove the point, she pulled gently on one particularly intractable piece of leather and saw, to her delight, that the entire tangle disappeared.

"Ta-da!" she announced.

While Lisa was introducing Alice to Comanche in a nearby stall, Max dropped his voice to speak confidentially to Stevie and Carole.

"Listen, keep an eye on Alice, will you? She may need some friends."

"Sure Max, no problem," Stevie said. "We always like to help newcomers anyway."

"Great," Max said. "Now you can feel like you've

2

earned your vacation. See you in class," he said, and then disappeared around a corner.

Carole sighed as she continued unknotting the leathers. She wasn't sure she wanted to be reminded about vacation. This was Tuesday. She and her father were leaving for five days in Florida on Saturday. It was going to be fun, because they'd be staying with family and there were so many great things to do in Florida. The problem was that it meant she might not do any riding for almost a week. The thought made Carole cringe. It was her midwinter break, and if she weren't going away, it would be easy to ride every single day. She definitely felt torn about going.

As Lisa and Alice headed for the tack room, Lisa saw the look on Carole's face and immediately knew something was bothering her. After all, they were The Saddle Club—and that not only meant that they were three horse-crazy girls, it meant they were best friends. In fact, one of the main requirements for membership in The Saddle Club was that the girls had to be willing to help one another when help was needed. Lisa had a feeling that this was one of those times. She gave Carole a sympathetic look and made a mental note to check in with her friend after class. Right now she had a job to do, and that was helping Alice Jackson with her horse.

"You're going to love Comanche," Lisa said to the new rider. "I've ridden him, and he's got some wonderful gaits, though he can be a little headstrong. You must be a pretty good rider if Max is putting you on Comanche for your first ride at Pine Hollow. Have you ridden a lot? I ride a lot, though I just started a couple of years ago. My friends Stevie and Carole— the girls you just met—are better riders than I am, but I do love learning, and Max says I'm doing well. Did he give you a test ride? He made me take a test ride when I started."

Lisa was prepared to ask a few more questions, but she realized that Alice was laughing. "I'm chattering, aren't I?" Lisa asked.

Alice nodded.

"I'm just trying to be helpful," Lisa said, now a little embarrassed.

"I know," Alice said. "And you *are* being helpful. Everything you can tell me about the horses and the stable will be useful. So keep on doing it. One thing, though—"

"What's that?"

"When you ask a question, why don't you pause a second and let me answer it?"

"It's a deal," Lisa said. She smiled and they shook hands on it.

In the tack room Lisa showed Alice where Comanche's tack was stowed. Alice carried the saddle, Lisa the bridle to Comanche's stall. Together the girls tacked up the horse.

As the girls talked, Alice's initial shyness seemed to melt away. Lisa found she liked Alice a lot. It turned out that Alice had actually done a lot of riding. She lived in Ohio and was on her school midwinter break. She was visiting her grandmother in Willow Creek, Virginia, where Lisa and her friends lived.

"To tell you the truth, I'd rather be home," Alice said. "But it's been sort of a nightmare there recently. My parents are fighting all the time. I think they're going to get a divorce, and they just don't want me to hear them scream at each other. They think I don't know how much they fight, and I don't want to let them know how much I do know. It's awful, Lisa. Really."

Lisa felt terrible for Alice. Lisa thought the most awful thing in the world would be to have her parents divorce. She got an unhappy tingling in her stomach just thinking about it. If she felt that way when it wasn't true, how must Alice feel when it was? A lump rose in her throat. She swallowed hard. There must be something she could do to help her.

"I don't mean to bore you," Alice added, when she noticed Lisa's faraway look.

"It's not boring," Lisa assured her. "I was just thinking. But we'd better get back to work. We've got to get this girth tight before class. See if you can distract Comanche so he doesn't take his usual gigantic deep breath before I pull on the girth. He usually tries to fool me about how tight it is. It used to work, but I've gotten wise."

Alice laughed. It was an easy laugh and made Lisa glad that she'd changed the subject. Maybe that was the one thing she really could do for Alice, who spoke then. "The horses I ride try that deep-breathing trick, too. Let's see if we can't outfox him."

Alice began petting Comanche's head and talking to him soothingly. Lisa patiently watched the horse's belly for signs of breathing. A girth didn't hurt a horse, but it was sometimes uncomfortable for a few minutes when it was first tightened. That was why some horses played games, taking in a deep breath while it was tightened and then letting it out so the girth felt loose. This time, though, the riders outfooled the horse. Comanche was enjoying Alice's attention so much, he didn't even notice while Lisa pulled the girth snugly.

"Success!" Lisa announced. The girls exchanged

high fives, finished the tacking-up process, and then walked the horse to the stable door.

Lisa always enjoyed showing new riders around Pine Hollow and introducing them to the stable's many traditions. One of the stable's traditions was that old riders showed new ones around. Another was that everybody worked. Traditions like these helped keep costs down for everybody, and the riders' parents liked that a lot.

"This is Barq, the horse I'm riding today," Lisa said. She opened the stall door and took the reins of the bay with a jagged white streak running down his face. "Barq is part Arabian, and his name means 'lightning' in Arabian. Isn't that neat?"

"Yes," Alice agreed. "He's a beauty, too." Lisa watched while Alice introduced herself to Barq, rubbing his soft nose gently. Lisa approved. This girl definitely knew about horses.

"Are you staying for the jump class?" Lisa asked.

"Oh, no," Alice said quickly.

"It's right after the flat class," said Lisa. "Max is just going to go over some basic techniques for about fifteen minutes."

"No, I can't," said Alice.

Lisa was surprised by how quickly Alice had said no. Maybe Alice was worried about how much it would cost to stay for a second class, or she was concerned that her jumping ability wouldn't be the same as the other students' in the class. Lisa decided she could set Alice's mind at ease on both those points. She could even do it diplomatically.

"The nice thing about the jump class today is that because it's going to be short, Max isn't even charging anybody for it. Also, one of our traditions here is that people of all levels work together in classes. Carole, who is really good, takes the same jump class that I do. You'll fit in. I'm sure."

"Thanks anyway," Alice said.

Lisa had the feeling a door had just been closed in her face, politely but firmly. She didn't have time right then to figure out what had happened, but she wasn't about to just let it drop. One thing she was sure of was that Alice would love Max's jump classes. He made them so much fun that Lisa and her friends rarely realized how hard they worked and how much they learned. Also, jumping was so much fun that it would help keep Alice's mind off her troubles.

As soon as class started, Lisa knew that she was right about Alice's skills. The girl definitely knew what she was doing on a horse. Comanche behaved perfectly. That, as much as anything, was an indication of how good a rider Alice was. Comanche was a great horse, but he had an independent streak that made him a bad choice for an inexperienced rider. A good rider, like Alice, knew how to explain to the horse exactly which one of them was in charge. Comanche wasn't questioning that. Alice was in charge.

Max had the class working on balance techniques. It wasn't easy. They had to ride without stirrups and sometimes even with their arms crossed, directing their horses simply with leg movements. One of the things Lisa had realized early in her riding lessons was how important balance was. A horse relied on the rider's balance to convey information. When a rider bounced around in the saddle, it could confuse the horse. She concentrated on improving her technique.

When the class was over, Max called for a five-minute cool-down period before the short jump class began. Most of the riders were staying for the jump class and took those five minutes to circle the schooling ring at a walk and let their horses relax.

Lisa saw Alice head for the exit. She wished Alice would stay for the class—maybe if she tried reassuring her one more time . . . Lisa gave Barq a little kick and hurried over to her new friend.

"You can stay, you know," Lisa said.

"No," Alice said. "I have to go."

Lisa tried again. "Some of the riders are new jumpers. Some are pretty experienced, just like in the flat class. We all just work together. . . ."

"I don't jump," Alice said flatly. She clearly didn't want to discuss it any further.

"Will you be at the next class on Saturday?" Lisa asked.

"Sure," Alice said. "I already told my grandmother about it. She'll get me here on time."

"See you then," Lisa said. "And it was nice meeting you."

"Nice meeting you, too. And, thanks for the help."

Alice dismounted and walked Comanche into the stabling area. As she walked off, Lisa wondered what she might have done to convince Alice to join the jump class. Then she decided she'd done everything she could have done by herself. But perhaps three heads would be better than one. Perhaps she could enlist the help of The Saddle Club. She knew her friends would agree that jumping could be the perfect antidote to Alice's unhappy family situation.

"Are you joining us?" Max asked sarcastically, bringing Lisa out of her thoughts.

Lisa glanced at her watch. It was exactly five minutes and three seconds since Max had announced a five-minute cool-down. That man could sure be specific when it came to class times!

Fifteen minutes and three seconds later, Stevie, Carole, and Lisa made a plan for a Saddle Club meeting. They often gathered after class at TD's—an ice-cream place at the nearby shopping center. Inside the stable Lisa noticed that Comanche had been untacked and groomed and there was no sign of Alice. As she walked with her friends to TD's, she told them about the new girl.

"She seemed awfully nice, but a little shy," Stevie said. Compared to Stevie, everybody in the world was shy.

"Her parents might be getting a divorce or something," Lisa said. "It wasn't too clear, but it sounds like it's bad news. She's here visiting her grandmother for vacation."

"Well," Carole said, "at least she's able to ride. Riding is always a good thing to do when times are tough." Her friends were aware that Carole knew what she was talking about. Her mother had died a few years earlier, and she'd often found comfort in being able to ride.

Then Lisa told her friends about how Alice seemed to be afraid of jumping.

11

"That doesn't make any sense," Stevie said. "She's a really good rider. Of course she can jump!"

"Something's keeping her from it," Lisa said. "And I'd like to know what it is."

"Me, too," Stevie said.

"Well, we're not going to find out here," Carole said, opening the door to TD's. "So we might as well get down to the serious business of ordering our sundaes." She led the way to their favorite table in the back of the restaurant, and the three of them slipped into their usual seats. Carole and Lisa each picked up a menu to study the options. Stevie seemed to know exactly what she wanted already.

That made Carole and Lisa a little nervous. Stevie was well-known for ordering very outrageous combinations. Her friends suspected she did it so nobody would want to take tastes of her sundaes. It also had something to do with trying to shock the waitress. It was a game they played. Stevie usually managed to win it.

"Who is it you're staying with in Florida?" Lisa asked Carole when she'd made up her mind.

"Dad's sister, Joanna," Carole said. "Then there's an Uncle Willie, and I have a cousin as well. Her name is Sheila. She's sixteen years old."

"Isn't she a rider, too?" Stevie said. She was crin-

12

kling her brows, trying to recall exactly what Carole had said. When it came to horses, she usually had a pretty good memory.

"She's got a pony," Carole reminded Stevie. "She's had him for years, and she rides him every day. She's as horse crazy as we are. It's one of the reasons I love her a lot. Also, like me, she wants to work with horses when she finishes school. The difference between us is that she's decided exactly what she wants to do already. She wants to be a trainer." Carole's friends knew that Carole couldn't make up her mind whether she wanted to be a trainer, instructor, breeder, show rider, owner, or veterinarian. At the moment, she wanted to be all of them.

"Well, if she rides, won't you get to ride, too?" Lisa asked.

"I don't know," Carole said. "That's what I was thinking about before class. When you're visiting other people, you really have to do what they want to do. I'm not sure Sheila's going to want to ride while I'm there, though I hope she will. Besides, she only has one horse and it's a *pony*," Carole added. "It's a little pony, and my cousin is big."

"Does she hurt the pony?" Lisa asked, concerned.

"Oh, no," Carole said. "It's a strong pony, and she's

not all that big, just regular sixteen-year-old size. But if she wants to succeed in competitions, she ought to have a regular-size horse."

"Does she want to succeed?" Stevie asked. It was hard to imagine that anybody wouldn't want to win prizes, but then she remembered that the girls had a friend named Kate Devine who had won a lot of prizes in horse shows and then decided she didn't want to compete anymore. She just wanted to ride. Maybe that was what this Sheila wanted, too.

"I'm not sure," Carole said. "I do know that she loves this pony so much that she's willing to do poorly in the shows because of it."

That sounded very odd to Stevie and Lisa.

"Not wanting to compete is one thing," Lisa said. "Wanting to lose is another altogether."

"Crazy," Stevie observed. "Plain crazy." Then her eyes lit up in a way her friends recognized. It meant a light bulb had just gone on. Stevie had an idea. "That's it!" she declared. "You'll be the perfect person to talk her into getting a new horse, Carole. All you have to do is explain what's going to happen."

"I've thought about that," Carole admitted. "But maybe it's not really my business what horse she rides.

14

Besides, she loves that pony, and she always has a good time riding it. What good would it do to have her give up the pony she loves for a horse she doesn't love, just to win ribbons?"

"Maybe she should have two horses," Stevie suggested. She was good at compromises, especially when it involved spending other people's money!

"And maybe pigs should fly," Lisa said wistfully. To her, owning one horse seemed like such a distant dream that she couldn't imagine owning two.

Her thoughts were interrupted by the arrival of the waitress. "You girls ready to order?" The waitress asked all of them, but she was looking at Stevie.

"Vanilla frozen yogurt," Carole said.

"Small hot fudge on chocolate ice cream," Lisa said.

The waitress wrote down their orders, but never took her eyes off Stevie. It was part of the challenge. Everybody there knew it. Would Stevie be able to come up with something so outrageous that the waitress would make a face?

Stevie took a deep breath.

"One scoop of Oreo cream, one of pistachio. Hot butterscotch. Pineapple topping. Each on both.

15

Whipped cream. Walnuts. Maraschino cherries. One on each."

The waitress wrote busily. Her face was stony.

"Oh, and can I have that chewy blueberry granola topping, too?"

The waitress's jaw dropped.

Stevie had won.

2

"Do you know what Aunt Joanna has planned for us this week?" Carole asked her father.

The two of them were sitting in their comfortable seats on the airplane. It was Saturday morning, and the plane was beginning its descent into the Florida airport, where their vacation awaited them.

"If I know my sister, whatever it is, it involves trying to introduce me to a very eligible woman," Colonel Hanson said, sighing with resignation.

"She's been trying to marry you off to one of her friends ever since Mom died," Carole said. "She's relentless, isn't she?"

"Absolutely. Every time I've seen her in the past

17

few years, we've somehow managed to run into a couple of her single friends."

"Is it embarrassing?"

"Not really. I suppose it's flattering, but it never seems to work out."

"Why don't you just tell Aunt Joanna to stop?" Carole asked. "You can find your own dates. I mean, it seems to me that you go out a couple of times a week at home without any help from her at all."

"I wouldn't want to interfere," Colonel Hanson explained. "She's having too much fun trying to fix me up."

"And what about Mrs. Dana?" she asked. Mrs. Dana was the mother of a girl Carole had befriended and helped. Her father and Mrs. Dana had seen a lot of one another since Carole introduced them. Carole liked her. Apparently her father did, too.

"I'm seeing her after we get back," Colonel Hanson said. "I've got tickets to a Beach Boys concert. She's almost as crazy about golden oldies as I am."

"Well, I'll tell you what," Carole said. "Every time Aunt Joanna tries to push one of her ever-so-slightly weird friends on you, I'll talk about Mrs. Dana. Is that a deal?"

"Deal," her father said. They shook on it. "But don't expect it to stop Joanna from trying."

18

Carole knew that was true. Her aunt could be very persistent when she decided to meddle. It wasn't Carole's favorite side of the woman.

A few hours later Carole found herself appreciating one of Aunt Joanna's better sides. Carole was standing in Aunt Joanna's kitchen, next to her cousin, Sheila. The two of them were taking turns using the food processor to make cole slaw. Carole was on cabbage, Sheila in charge of carrots. Aunt Joanna had orchestrated an entire work crew, including the girls, Colonel Hanson, and Uncle Willie. Everybody had a job; everybody was enjoying the work.

"Where's your dill weed, Joanna?" Colonel Hanson asked. "I can't make a marinade for the shrimp without dill weed."

Aunt Joanna produced a whole tray of spices. "Here you go, Mitch," she said. "Create!" His eyes lit up. Aunt Joanna went on. "You're a wonderful cook, Mitch. Some woman would be really lucky—"

Carole knew a cue when she heard one. "That's just what Mrs. Dana says about him," she piped in.

"—to catch you," Aunt Joanna finished, apparently unaware of Carole's none-too-subtle hint. "But remember to make a lot of marinade, because we've got a lot of shrimp, because there are going to be a lot of people at the party tomorrow. And it had better be delicious."

The party, Carole had learned, was to be a family reunion. She had many relatives who lived in the area, most of whom she'd never met, and the rest of whom she didn't know very well, but all of whom she was sure she'd like. Her father's family was large and boisterous. It was always fun to be with them.

"They're all relatives, Joanna," Colonel Hanson said. "How fussy can they be?"

"Not all of them are relatives," Aunt Joanna said. "There are a few special nonfamily guests."

"Like who?" Uncle Willie asked. He was suspicious.

"Oh, just a few," Aunt Joanna said vaguely. "Well, like there's a friend of mine who didn't have anything planned for tomorrow, and so I thought—"

"A single friend?" Uncle Willie asked. He knew what Aunt Joanna was up to.

"Well, I guess so," Aunt Joanna said. "I think she said something about her son spending the weekend with her ex, and I'm just sure everybody in the family will like her, so I said we'd pick her up on the way over to Julie's."

Carole tried again. "Dad, didn't you ask me to remind you to call Mrs. Dana so she'd know we got here safely?"

Her father smiled. "Thanks, hon," he said. "I'll take care of it."

That, Carole knew, was her father's way of saying he could manage, and he didn't want to upset his sister or give her the impression that he was wildly in love with Mrs. Dana. Carole realized that if Aunt Joanna thought that was the case, it would just invite another kind of interference. It was hard to know how to balance in a case like this. She decided to change the subject instead.

"Could somebody please tell me again what all these events are that you guys scheduled for me and Dad? I thought this was supposed to be a peaceful vacation!"

"Sure," Sheila obliged. "Tomorrow's the family reunion. Then Monday the five of us are going to Disney World for the day. Then Tuesday I've arranged for you to borrow a horse, and the two of us are going to have a picnic on the beach. We'll ride to this beautiful place I know where there's a patch of coral you won't believe, and I've got snorkels for us—"

"That beach can be dangerous, you know," Uncle Willie said. "If there's a riptide, you could be in trouble."

"Dad," Sheila said. "I was practically born in the water down here. I can handle it."

21

"You can't handle a riptide," Uncle Willie said.

"No, but I can stay out of one," said Sheila. "Don't worry. We'll be really careful. Besides, there's just about always a lifeguard on duty. We'll be fine. I promise."

"If you want to ride, you'd be better off riding at the school," Aunt Joanna said. There was a little irritation in her voice that Carole wasn't used to hearing. "Carole could help you try riding some of the horses that Mr. Abelman said were for sale."

"Mother," Sheila said. Aunt Joanna wasn't about to stop now, though.

"I mean it, Sheila," she said. "You really ought to let us sell that pony. You're never going to succeed as a competitive rider if you're riding Maverick."

"I don't care about succeeding as a competitive rider," Sheila said. "I want to ride Maverick, and I won't let you sell him."

"Carole, will you talk some sense into this girl's head?" Aunt Joanna asked. "Tell her that if she wants to be a horse professional, she's going to have to have some ribbons on her walls. She's going to have to have a way to show the world that she knows how to train a horse."

"Maverick is very well trained," Sheila said.

"Sure he is, but you never win any ribbons riding

22

him! And your father and I pay to feed and house him month after month. We're not getting anything for our money, and neither are you."

This sounded like an argument that Sheila and her mother had had before, and would have again.

"Who wants to taste my marinade?" Colonel Hanson asked. Four hands went up. Everybody was glad to have the focus of the conversation switched to something noncontroversial, like how many peppercorns the marinade needed.

STEVIE LOOKED DEEP into the horse's eyes. The horse looked back into hers.

"I think Starlight misses Carole already," Stevie said to Lisa, who was standing right next to her.

"Maybe," Lisa said. "Although she was here just yesterday."

"Yes, but that was yesterday," Stevie said.

"Well, absence makes the heart grow fonder. Since Carole is going to be away for five days, Starlight is going to adore her when she gets back. In the meantime, it's our job to take care of him, right?"

"Right," Stevie agreed. She gave Starlight a pat and a hug and then promised him she'd be right back. She went to get some fresh hay and some grain. Lisa took his bucket for water.

Stevie and Lisa were only too happy to take care of Starlight. He was a wonderful horse, and Carole was their best friend. Feeding him and mucking out his stall wasn't really hard work. It was fun. Since they were on school vacation, they were going to be at the stable every day anyway, and this was just one small extra chore for them. It was no problem.

In the feed room, Stevie picked up a flake of hay in one hand and a coffee can of grain with the other. That was Starlight's breakfast. He nuzzled her happily as she doled out the goodies in his stall. He also sniffed at the fresh water Lisa supplied.

"I think we have a happy customer," Lisa observed. She offered her hand for Stevie to shake.

"Good morning!" Alice greeted them cheerfully. "This is your friend's horse, isn't it?"

"Yes, this is Starlight," Stevie introduced them. "Carole is away for a couple of days, so we're horse-sitting."

"Lucky horse, I think—"

"And lucky Carole to own him," said Lisa. "He's a great horse, and she's made him even greater by all the work she's done with him."

Alice nodded. "I was watching her in class," she

said. "She's wonderful with him. He's obviously got a lot of potential, and she saw to it that he did his best with every single move. It was like she wasn't going to let him get away with anything. I thought it was funny when he took two steps backward, and she made him take two forward. Then he took one backward, and she made him take one forward. She's always in charge."

"It's important," Lisa said.

"I know it is," said Alice. "I used to ride a horse who always wanted to be in charge. When the instructor had us all turn our horses around, my horse wanted to turn around in the opposite direction from the way the other horses in the class were turning. At first I thought it was funny, and it didn't matter. But when he got the idea that he could do what he wanted to do, I lost all control. He stopped paying attention to everything I said. The instructor got so angry with me that he excused me from the class. I learned my lesson. And that was four years ago. I've never forgotten it."

Lisa and Stevie smiled. That was a lesson every rider seemed to need to know. And they all learned it the same way!

"Say, would you like to ride Starlight?" Stevie asked suddenly.

"Me?" Alice asked.

"Sure," Stevie said. "See, Carole's away until Wednesday, and Starlight's got to get some exercise, but Lisa and I each want to ride other horses in class today. It's not that we don't love Starlight. We do. It's just that I'm kind of in the middle of working on something with Topside, and Lisa here has been trying to ride Barq as much as possible so she can get used to him—"

"Pepper, the horse I used to ride has been retired," Lisa explained. Alice nodded.

"—so you'd really be doing us and Carole a favor if you'd ride Starlight. He's a little too independent for the average rider. But you're not an average rider. I'm sure Carole would be glad."

"And I'm sure Max would approve," Lisa said. It was like Stevie to ignore the fact that they'd have to get his approval, and it was like Lisa to remember it.

"And I'm sure I'd love it," Alice said. "Definitely yes. I'll get his tack."

"And I'll get Max's okay," said Lisa.

"And I'll get Topside tacked up so I can be on time to class!"

There was a flurry of activity then, which resulted in the three girls meeting at the good-luck horseshoe for the final preparation before class. Max was there, too.

"I watched you in class, Alice, and I know you're a good rider. Starlight has a bit of a mind of his own, though. You have to be a little careful."

"I will be. I promise," Alice said. "Besides, I always am that."

"She'll do fine," Stevie said. "As a matter of fact, Max, I'm so sure she'll do fine that I think she should come along on the trail ride that Lisa and I are planning to take this afternoon."

Lisa thought she saw Max suppressing a smile. Stevie had a way of taking a small "yes," such as getting permission for Alice to ride Starlight in class, and turning it into a big "yes."

"We'll see how she does in class," Max said.

"Okay," Stevie said. That was clearly as close as she was going to get to a yes, big or small.

But Alice was shaking her head. "I can't do it," she said. "I have to do something with my grandmother this afternoon."

Max seemed a little bit relieved to have the question removed.

"Tomorrow?" Stevie pressed.

"Great!" said Alice.

"Maybe," said Max. Then he looked at his watch.

That was a sure sign that they should all stop talking and get into class.

Red O'Malley was teaching the young riders' class that morning. He began the class by having the riders go through all their gaits. Then he repeated some of the balance exercises that they'd been working on Tuesday. During riding class, as with every class that Lisa ever took, her whole attention was on the teacher and her own performance. That was one of the reasons why she was a straight-A student.

That was not the case with Stevie. She listened to Red and followed his instructions, but her lively and active mind just couldn't be totally occupied with one thing at a time—not when there were so many other things to think about at the same time! That included things like admiring Lisa's total concentration and watching Alice to see if she was as good as they thought she was. She was. Alice had complete control of Starlight, and she had done it without any apparent effort. Stevie knew that was the hardest part —working hard and making it look as if you weren't. A horse responded to leadership like that. Starlight was working as well with Alice as he did with Carole, and that was something Stevie could really appreciate. There was no doubt left in Stevie's mind. Alice was a really good rider.

One of the other things that got Stevie's attention was the fact that Max was watching the class from the door to the ring. His eyes never left Alice, and a smile never left his face. Stevie knew for sure, then, that he'd let Alice go on the trail ride on Sunday. That made Stevie feel good. It confirmed her own feelings about Alice's skills. It also was a proven fact, demonstrated by The Saddle Club, that it was always more fun to ride with three people than two. That was just one more reason why she was glad Alice would be there the next day.

Stevie was so pleased by all these thoughts that her attention totally left Red O'Malley. That was why she didn't hear him tell the riders to halt and line up. It came to Stevie's attention only when she realized that she was circling the ring alone with her feet out of the stirrups and eight other members of the class laughing at her. Sheepishly, she drew Topside to a halt at the end of the line.

"We're going to try another exercise now," Red said. Next to him there was a pile of orange cones— like the ones used on highways to redirect traffic. "I'm going to make you an obstacle course. You're going to be moving back and forth quickly, changing directions, first at the walk, then the trot. It's a way you can use what you've learned about balance, because every time you shift directions, you're going to have to rebalance yourselves."

Then he began dealing out the cones. If the girls had been on skis, Stevie might have called it a slalom course. Red certainly expected them to handle a lot of turns. And then she saw that it wasn't all exactly lateral, because he put some cavalletti on the course, too. Those were long poles that the horses would have to jump over. Red put them on low risers so they were only about six inches off the ground. Stevie thought this would be fun. Balance was important when you were on a flat course, but it was absolutely critical when you were jumping. She hoped she was going to be able to use the skills she'd been practicing.

"Okay, begin with the start of the line," Red said. "Lisa!"

Lisa looked over the course carefully. There were eight sets of cones she had to navigate and then three small jumps at the end. Before she began riding, she imagined her way through the course and over all the jumps. The only tricky part was figuring out how many strides there would be between the little jumps. Her eyes told her the answer was three.

Lisa nodded—mostly to assure herself she was ready —and then she began. She maneuvered through the

31

pairs of cones smoothly, very much aware of the way her horse moved through the turns, as well as the way she compensated for the shifting directions, keeping her weight evenly distributed as they proceeded. That, she understood, was balance. She was doing it.

Then there were the three little jumps. They really were just high steps for a horse, and at a walk, that was just how Barq treated them.

"Good," Red said. "Next!"

Next was Alice. She and Starlight did the whole course very well and very smoothly. She was such a good rider, Lisa thought, she probably didn't even think about turns and balance. She just did it naturally. Then Lisa watched Alice approach the three low jumps. All the confidence she'd had through the cone part of the course seemed to disappear. She leaned over to one side and glared at the small obstacles, slowing Starlight to a very cautious walk. She went over one of the poles, stopped, looked ahead, and then moved her horse forward to the next. She repeated the stop and cautious forward movement for the third.

"Nice," Red said, though a slight look of concern crossed his face.

The rest of the riders completed the course as well,

including Stevie. Stevie understood that it wasn't meant to be a difficult course. It was meant only to make the rider aware of shifting for balance. She and Topside completed it without incident.

"Now, at a rising trot," Red said.

Lisa led off. It was trickier at a trot, but the practice at a walk had taught her a lot. Also, Barq seemed to understand what was expected, so Lisa could concentrate on her balance and let Barq take care of his own —with a few reminders from her.

When she finished the eight turns and approached the three poles, all the hard work was done. The only thing now was to jump the poles. Barq knew what to do. So did Lisa. She rose in the saddle and leaned forward, keeping her balance centered over the horse, and he lifted himself over each of the very low jumps. When they had finished the third, Lisa sat down in the saddle again and brought Barq to a walk, joining the end of the line.

"Very good, Lisa," Red said. Then he turned to Alice. "Next," he invited her.

Alice started Starlight trotting. She managed to get him to take the turns so smoothly that it looked as if he were flowing through the course. She never appeared to move. She was really good! Then when she finished the turns and came to the poles,

33

she drew Starlight to a walk and went over the three poles, one at a time, much as she had the first time.

This was odd. Stevie didn't understand it, and neither did Lisa. Neither, apparently, did Red.

"Good, but what happened at the poles?" Red asked Alice.

"I went over them," she answered, almost defensively.

"Yes," Red agreed. "You did. But you broke your gait."

"I don't jump," she said.

"But you're—"

"I don't jump," she repeated.

"I see," said Red. "Next!"

Something was strange, and both Lisa and Stevie knew it. It was one thing not to jump, but those six-inch poles were hardly a jump, and a rider with as much skill on the flat as Alice had certainly shouldn't be spooked by a six-inch obstacle.

If anyone else in the class had done that, Red would have stopped and taken the time to review the technique for going over small obstacles. With Alice, however, because it was so odd, and because she was really just visiting for a few classes, Red seemed reluctant to do anything.

"She doesn't know what she's missing," Stevie whispered to Lisa.

Lisa nodded. "I tried to get her to come to jump class on Tuesday—"

"Next!" Red barked at the next rider in line.

"We've got to do something about it," Stevie whispered.

"Like what?" Lisa hissed back.

"Something," Stevie said.

Lisa could have sworn then that she could hear wheels turning in Stevie's head. A scheme was forming.

WHEN CLASS WAS over, Stevie and Lisa helped Alice untack Starlight and groom him. Although the tradition at Pine Hollow was that each rider was responsible for the horse that she was riding, Stevie and Lisa felt a special obligation to Starlight since they were supposed to be taking care of him while Carole was away.

The girls chattered about horses, riding classes, and Starlight. The one thing they didn't chatter about was the fact that Alice had refused to go over the small obstacles. It was all Stevie could do to keep from asking about it, but she knew she and Lisa needed to talk about it first, and they would have a chance to do that soon when they went on their own trail ride.

When the last bit of work was done for Starlight, the three of them set a time to meet for their ride the next day, and Alice waved good-bye. Her grandmother was waiting for her, she explained. Then she was gone.

"We need to talk," Stevie said.

Lisa grinned. "I know. I can tell by the look in your eye that you're up to something."

"But not here." Stevie loved being mysterious.

"Then where?"

"On the trail."

There was no need to say any more. Stevie and Lisa had each brought a brown-bag lunch. They retrieved them from the old refrigerator where Max kept sodas and other drinks for his riders. The girls each took a container of fruit juice. Stevie put both their lunches in her backpack, slipped that over her shoulders, and then they brought their horses to the door of the stable. The girls mounted, touched the good-luck horseshoe for the second time that day, and aimed themselves toward the woods.

Lisa loved trail rides. She liked classes and shows, too, but most of all she liked to ride on trails. She loved being outdoors, and something about the combination of woods and horses seemed just perfect. Their class had been in the outdoor ring, but it was one thing to be in a ring, another to be in the freedom of the woods. She took a deep breath and sighed contentedly.

"Feels good, doesn't it?" Stevie asked.

"Wonderful," Lisa agreed.

The trails behind Pine Hollow all started out in the fields, but most of them wound up in the forested area about a quarter of a mile away. There were wonderful places to ride there, and dozens of trails that every Pine Hollow rider soon learned and soon learned to love.

Stevie was in the lead. The girls walked their horses for the first quarter mile or so until they were warmed up, then they began trotting. Stevie chose a trail through the woods that wound in all different directions while it took the riders uphill and then down, leading to the creek that had given their town its name, Willow Creek.

The winding part of the trail was great. Lisa found she could practice everything they had been working on in class.

"Red would love our doing this!" she said to Stevie.

"Red suggested it!" Stevie said back.

That made sense. At Pine Hollow the instructors

were always trying to find ways to connect the skills
the riders worked on in one kind of riding with another kind of riding. This was a natural opportunity to
do just that.

Stevie was enjoying the ride just as much as Lisa
was. The only drawback to trail riding was that when
you were trotting or cantering, it was hard to talk, but
she had a plan in mind. She was headed for a rock
that sat by the edge of the creek. They could tie up
their horses nearby and have a picnic lunch. It was
still too early in the season for them to dangle their
feet in the creek. It was the only thing about this trail
ride that wasn't perfect as far as Stevie was concerned.

Max saw to it that all the trails around Pine Hollow
were kept clear and safe for the riders, but he couldn't
always keep up with nature on that score. Today, for
instance, Stevie spotted a small tree trunk that had
fallen across the trail. It wasn't a problem. In fact, it
was just a great opportunity for an unexpected jump.
She waved to Lisa to make sure she'd seen it as well,
and then, when she knew Lisa would know what to
do, she signaled Topside to canter across the smooth
ground between where they were and the tree. Topside was only too happy to oblige. It wasn't much of a
jump—less than two feet—but jumping at any height
was fun for Stevie. Topside seemed to agree. The two

of them flew over the obstacle and landed smoothly. Stevie kept Topside going for a few more feet and then drew him to a halt and turned to watch her friend. When you were jumping it was very important that somebody else was watching. Lisa had watched her from behind. Now Stevie watched Lisa from ahead.

"Oh, that was great!" Lisa said. "It's like Red planned some more practice for us on this trail and laid that thing there just for us."

"Not likely," Stevie said. "But whatever happened, I'm glad. Going over natural jumps like that reminds me of the fox hunt. Remember?"

Lisa did. They'd had a wonderful time fox hunting. The big difference between a fox hunt and a trail ride was that with a fox hunt, the riders weren't even following trails. That could be wild!

The girls walked their horses then for a while, because they were approaching the creek and they wanted the horses to have a chance to cool down before they stopped for lunch.

Lisa drew Barq up alongside Stevie and Topside so that they could talk as the horses walked. She was still feeling exhilarated from the jump and couldn't stop wondering about Alice's reluctance to do it in class.

"I wonder if Alice has ever even tried to jump,"

Lisa mused, "or if she's had a bad experience with it. Maybe she's just afraid. Some people have fears that don't make any sense, you know."

"Like my fear of exams?" Stevie said.

"Not exactly. Your fear of exams isn't irrational. See, if you don't keep up with your homework and if you don't pay attention in class—" There was an impish look on Lisa's face.

"Spare me! I'm on vacation," Stevie said, laughing.

"Sure, but anyway, it's not the same thing as it is with Alice. Somehow, for some reason, she's convinced that she shouldn't jump. I wonder if it could be connected with her family situation—like maybe she's afraid of what's happening with her parents and that makes her afraid of other things, too, like jumping?"

Stevie thought about this for a minute. "Maybe," she said. "It's a little bit like what happens when I get angry at one of my brothers. Suddenly I'm angry at all of them."

Lisa knew this was true. Stevie had three brothers, and it seemed that she was always at war with at least one of them. Also, Stevie spent so much time getting into trouble that the rest of her time seemed to be spent avoiding her parents because of the hot water she was already in.

"Actually," Stevie went on, "my family is very important to me. I've been trying to think how I would feel if my parents were fighting all the time and were talking about getting a divorce. To tell you the truth, it's the scariest thought I've ever had. I . . ."

Stevie's voice faltered as she contemplated what it would be like to be in Alice's position. She tried to go on, but it was hard. The ideas were so big and so awful, she couldn't even get her mind around them.

"I just don't know," Stevie said finally, knowing she hadn't said at all what she felt.

"Me, neither," said Lisa. "But I know it's upsetting Alice, and I'd like to be able to help her. She's so nice."

"And such a good rider," Stevie added.

The girls drew their horses to a halt then and dismounted. They'd reached the creek, and they were ready for their picnic. The girls each snapped a lead rope onto their bridles and secured the lead ropes around the large branch of a tree by the creek, close enough to the water so the horses could have a cooling drink.

Stevie climbed the rock by the creek. Lisa joined her there. It took only a few minutes to fish the lunch bags out of Stevie's backpack, and their picnic began.

"I've been thinking," Stevie said.

"Good!" Lisa teased.

"About Alice," Stevie continued.

"Should we bring her here tomorrow when we go on our trail ride?" Lisa asked.

"Yes, I think so," Stevie agreed. "It's such a pretty place, even in this cool weather, that it always makes me feel better. It will probably have the same effect on her."

"Good idea."

"And I think we should bring her the same way we came," said Stevie more slowly, indicating that each word had some weight.

"The same way? But there's that—"

Tree, Lisa thought. There was a tree across the trail. She suddenly realized what Stevie was up to. It was the scheme Stevie had been working on before only now it was complete—and it was great! The trunk was a two-foot-high obstacle that any well-trained horse would simply jump over. An experienced rider would have no more trouble with it than she would with a six-inch-high-pole. "You want Alice to have to jump the tree!" Lisa exclaimed.

"It's going to be perfect," said Stevie. "It'll just be there. I'll be in front so she won't be able to see it until I've been over it, and I'll just be a few feet in front of her. Starlight's a wonderful horse. He's the best jumper in the stable. He won't be able to resist it, no matter what Alice says, especially if she doesn't have much warning."

"And I'll be behind her," said Lisa thoughtfully. "So in case anything does happen, I'll be right there. She's such a good rider, she's sure to react naturally to the jump, and she'll go over it smooth as glass."

"With some help from Starlight," said Stevie sensibly. "I wouldn't trust any other horse to do this, you know."

"I know. He's the perfect choice. Then, can you see it?" Lisa's mind began soaring with the possibilities. "Alice is sure to realize how silly she's been about jumping—that it's really a lot of fun and not dangerous. It's like we're opening up a whole new world of possibilities for her on horseback. She's going to love it!"

"It won't exactly make up for the fact that her parents are splitting," Stevie added.

"But it will give her something else to think about," Lisa concluded.

"That's important, too. When something bad is going on that you can't do anything about, you should have something good to distract you."

"And by the time she leaves here, she's going to be a super jumper!" Lisa felt warm and happy, and she knew Stevie felt the same way. It was great to think that they had a friend who had a problem and they could do something about it. That was what The Saddle Club did best, wasn't it? Now all they had to do was make sure that they did it right.

"We've got work to do," Lisa declared.

"Like what?"

"We've got to get back to where that tree is and make sure that it's not too visible from far ahead on the trail and that it's as low as we can make it so it will be totally safe for Alice. We have to make it so Starlight has lots of warning and Alice only has a little—just enough."

Stevie agreed. The girls finished their sandwiches and juice and spent the rest of the afternoon doctoring the "jump" to make it perfect for Alice. By the time they returned to Pine Hollow, they were totally satisfied with their work and so happy about what was going to happen tomorrow that they didn't even mind the scowl they got from Max, who reminded them that they'd been due back at the stable sometime earlier.

"We were doing you a favor, Max," Stevie assured him. "A tree had fallen across the creek trail, and we couldn't just leave it where it was."

"Oh, thank you," Max said, changing his tune completely. "Another rider told me about that tree. I was going to go out later today and move it."

"No need to," Stevie said quickly. "We moved it to a much safer place. And we'll be going out on that trail tomorrow. We'll check it again for you."

Lisa almost gagged. What Stevie said was true, of course, but what Max *heard* was something else altogether. They had moved the tree. They'd moved it so it would be more of a surprise for Alice, and they'd made it lower to the ground so it would be a safer jump, and they'd covered parts of it with leaves to camouflage it.

"Thanks, girls," Max said. "You could have just reminded me, and I would have done the work myself. I appreciate your help, though."

At his thanks Lisa and Stevie felt a twinge of guilt. But it passed quickly, for tomorrow they really would be doing two things for Max: first, moving the tree trunk completely off the trail, and then, bringing him a new jumping student—one with a little bit of experience!

5

"OH, CAROLE! How wonderful to see you!"

Carole looked at the woman, a total stranger to her, except for the fact that they were apparently related. For that, she got a hug.

"You've grown so!" said another person—cousin Fred, she thought.

"Isn't she the image of Mitch!"

"Oh, I don't think so. I think she's got Grandfather William's eyes. And her nose—well, that's the exact same as your brother's was."

Carole was quite befuddled. For one thing, she was starting to feel as if she'd been made of spare parts. For another, she couldn't remember anybody's name, and

47

they all remembered hers. Everyone also seemed to know things about her that she didn't know, like who her relatives were.

"Well, Carole, this is your second cousin Jack." Carole shook the young man's hand, not having the faintest idea how she'd ever gotten a second cousin. "He's Eloise's boy," Aunt Joanna said, as if that explained everything.

There were more than thirty relatives at the house, and Carole knew only a few of them. She swore to herself that she'd ask her father to help her construct a family tree that very evening so she could begin to understand where all these people came from.

Once Carole had been hugged by everybody there, it was time to work on the meal they would all share. Everybody seemed to want to pitch in and help on the food, and that made it even more confusing. Carole and Sheila carried a big vat of cole slaw between them, and somebody provided two large bowls for serving it. The two girls tilted the vat while somebody —cousin Eloise? or was it Elsa?—scooped it into the bowls.

"How many Hansons does it take to serve cole slaw?" Carole asked, mimicking the light-bulb jokes that had been so popular a while back.

"Oh, see! I told you! She's just like her father!"

48

cried out a cousin from the corner of the kitchen. "She loves old jokes, too!"

It seemed that today Carole wasn't even going to be allowed to call her sense of humor her own. She decided she should just relax and enjoy it.

Somebody handed Carole a plate of vegetables and dip and told her to find a place to put it. Carole took the plate to a table that wasn't completely overloaded and set it there. Then she sampled some of the cauliflower—her favorite, as long as it was raw. She never much liked it cooked. She was savoring the deliciously spicy dip when Aunt Joanna approached her with somebody she assumed was another long-lost relative. This time it was a woman about Aunt Joanna's age.

"Carole, I want you to meet Midge Ford," said Aunt Joanna, and then she disappeared, leaving Carole with the newest guest at the party.

Carole smiled broadly and reached out to give the woman what she'd come to understand was the standard family hug.

The woman returned the hug, but seemed a little surprised.

"How are we related?" Carole asked politely and braced herself for an explanation about Uncle Fritz's second wife's first cousin.

"We're not," Midge said. "I'm the one nonrelative here, I guess. Joanna just told me there was a get-together, and I should be here because there would be so many interesting people."

Then Carole remembered. This was the woman Joanna had invited for her father.

"I had no idea it was really a family reunion. I feel kind of awkward because I don't know anybody here —except Joanna and now you."

Carole said the first thing that popped into her mind. "Don't worry. I don't know anybody here, either. And I think a lot of them don't as well," she said, gesturing to the sea of relatives. "Just tell them that you're cousin Elbert's second daughter by his third wife, and they'll all hug you."

"Because nobody wants to admit they don't remember me?"

"Or cousin Elbert . . ."

Midge began laughing. She had a nice laugh. Carole liked that.

"The least I can do is carry my own weight here and pitch in to help. What needs to be done?" Midge asked.

Carole looked around. It seemed that just about every flat surface was covered with a food that was somebody's specialty. She also knew that the kitchen

was mobbed with relatives who were putting the fin-
ishing touches on something or other. There really
didn't seem to be anything to do, and she was telling
Midge this when her father approached.

"Hi, honey, how's it going?" he asked, giving her
yet another hug. Carole thought she was probably
into triple digits on hugs for the day already, but she
could never have enough of the ones that came from
her dad. She hugged him back.

She noticed that her father was looking at Midge
then, as if trying to place her. Carole decided to help.

"Dad, this is Midge Ford. She's cousin Elbert's second daughter by his third wife. . . ."

A confused look came across the Colonel's face,
and then it cleared. "Midge Ford," he said. "You're
Joanna's friend, aren't you? The one she's trying to fix
me up with?"

"Yes, I am," she said. "And you must be Mitch
Hanson—the 'single' brother she won't stop talking
about."

"Guilty," he said, offering her his hand. They
shook. "And I see you've already met my daughter."

"Yes, I have, and we've already had a laugh together."

"Well, then, let me introduce you to some more of
the family," Colonel Hanson said. "And did you try

51

the punch? I'm told that one bowl is alcohol free and the other has some of Edgar's homemade brew in it, but nobody will say which is which. Are you bold enough to try?"

"Definitely," said Midge. She laughed again and walked off with Carole's father.

Carole looked around for a few seconds, not sure which way to turn. She spotted Sheila then, surrounded by younger cousins. She didn't know for sure what they were talking about, but she heard words like "saddle" and "conformation" coming out of the group, so she was, naturally, drawn to it. Her suspicions were correct. They were talking about horses.

"But just exactly what *is* the difference between Western and Eastern riding?" one young cousin asked.

"English," Sheila said, correcting her automatically. "There are a lot of differences, which mostly have to do with their original purposes being different. A lot of English riding developed from military use of horses. Some, too, from use of horses in hunting. Western riding was all work—cattle work. The tack in each type of riding is different."

"And the horses, too, are they different?"

"Yes and no," Sheila said. It was a complicated question, and Carole could tell by the look on Sheila's face that she was eager to answer it.

Carole smiled. This was right up her alley, and Sheila seemed to be as interested in giving a complete answer as Carole herself would have been. Carole's friends sometimes teased her that she had many more complete answers than they did questions and she could go on and on a lot. She took their teasing good-naturedly, but it was a relief to be with someone who liked to share information as much as she did.

"Each breed of horse has distinct strengths," Sheila began. "English riders like to use Thoroughbreds or 'warmbloods' because they are so graceful and fast and such good jumpers. Cowboys would generally choose a quarter horse. They're admired for their bursts of speed, which come in handy chasing after dogies on the range. Then there are horses like the Morgans, who have incredible strength and endurance. . . ."

Carole was with her all the way. She added that Arabians were known for their endurance as well as their beauty, but on the Arabian desert, perhaps their finest trait was their ability to go without water for long periods of time.

"Not too long, though. Of course, they can become dehydrated, just like people can."

"And then there are draught horses that aren't really either English or Western, but are meant to pull loads—"

53

Suddenly Sheila and Carole looked at each other. They had lost their audience. All the younger kids had wandered away from them, drawn to another room by a new video game.

"Uh-oh," Sheila said.

"Don't worry. It happens to me all the time," Carole comforted her. "Nobody in the world cares about horses as much as I do—and my best friends, of course."

"Except me," said Sheila.

That was true. Even though the audience of younger kids was gone, it didn't mean Carole and Sheila couldn't talk about horses. So they did.

Sheila knew Carole's horse was named Starlight, but she didn't know much more about the horse. Carole took the opportunity to fill her in on all the wonderful details. Sheila had some suggestions about further training for the horse, but she certainly agreed that most of what Carole was doing was just right.

"Especially since it's working," Sheila concluded. "It is, isn't it?"

"It sure is," Carole agreed. "We were at a horse show not long ago, and we did very well. Came in second overall."

"That's great. My parents wish I could do that."

They were nearing a subject Carole was curious

54

about but didn't want to raise. She waited to see what else Sheila would share.

"Maverick and I are like one person," Sheila said. "We've been riding together for so long that I just can't imagine what it would be like to ride another horse. And I don't want to find out, either. I mean, I wouldn't mind riding another horse now and again, but I can't stand the idea that Maverick and I wouldn't be together again. I love him so much. . . ."

"Everybody! Everybody! May I have your attention, please!" It was Uncle Willie. The whole family quieted down for Uncle Willie's announcement. "It's time for a little softball game in the backyard. I'm captain of one of the teams. Mitch here claims he's too good to be a captain. He's going to be the colonel of the other!" There was laughter. "Everybody up for softball. We're going to choose up sides. Knowing which side my bread is buttered on, I call for Joanna first!"

Teams formed quickly and the game began. It was followed by some volleyball and then a wonderful meal. By the end of the day, as darkness fell, the family members turned to quieter moments and, finally, singing. Carole was surprised to find that there was a whole group of people who knew many of the same silly songs that her father had been teaching her since the first time she could sing. Her favorite was one about a little froggy who jumped from lily pad to lily pad all day long, accomplishing nothing at all. She always liked it when she and her dad sang it together. Now she found she liked it even better when thirty people sang it all at the same time. Even though she'd never met most of them, or didn't remember meeting them until today, they seemed to be bound together by more than the fortune of their births. They were bound by a family tradition that crossed generational lines, as well as state borders. This was family. Carole found she liked it.

When the last note had been sounded, and the last paper plate put in the last plastic bag, it was time to fold up the last of the chairs and get ready to go back to Aunt Joanna's.

Carole and Midge seemed to be the ones working on the chairs. Carole hadn't seen much of Midge since they'd left Joanna's house, but when she had seen her, she'd been near Mitch Hanson. Both her father and Midge seemed to be smiling a lot. It gave Carole a funny feeling. She loved her father and wanted him to be happy, but she felt a certain loyalty to Mrs. Dana. Yet she liked Midge. Still she didn't know how she would feel if her father actually married

somebody. Dating was one thing. Living with somebody else was another.

"I like your family," Midge said.

"So do I," Carole said.

"I hope I get to see more of them," said Midge.

"I hope you do, too," said Carole. She meant it,
too. And she found that even more confusing.

Carole had learned that there were some things in
life she wasn't going to understand, and these confused feelings were among them. She shrugged, picked
up the next chair, folded it, and handed it to Midge to
put on the pile. The reunion was over. She'd had a
wonderful time and met lots of relatives she liked.
She'd also met a nonrelative she liked. What was the
big deal about that?

Now it was time to start hugging people all over
again—this time to say good-bye. When the last hug
had been hugged, Carole and her dad climbed into
Uncle Willie's car for the drive home. Carole was exhausted. She fell asleep in the car, dreaming about
family, food, games, songs—and Midge Ford.

Stevie and Lisa were so excited about their secret that they could barely keep from telling Alice. But they knew, as they set out on their trail ride on Sunday, that Alice would find out soon enough.

"You're going to love the trails here," Stevie said to her. "They're beautiful, and fun to ride. They just always seem to have surprises for us, too."

"You mean you get lost?" Alice asked. She sounded a little nervous.

"No, we don't get lost," Lisa assured her. "Even if we did, the horses would always be able to find the way home. They're like the pigeons who always know where to go. The horses always know where to go to get food and water!"

It was true. More than one horse had brought an unwary rider back to the stables simply because the rider hadn't taken control of the horse. That wasn't going to happen with the three of them, though. Stevie and Lisa knew exactly where they were going.

It was fun for them to have a new rider to whom they could introduce all the wonderful things about Pine Hollow and the surrounding trails. The girls talked easily, with Stevie and Lisa filling Alice in on all the fun they'd been having riding at Pine Hollow.

They told her about the mock hunt and the fox hunt; they told her about the time they'd helped the police uncover a ring of horsenappers; they told her about the time the colt, Samson, had been stuck in the briars and Carole had rescued him.

"Remember the first time we took you on a trail ride?" Stevie asked Lisa.

She did. She remembered that they'd gone through a field that had a bull in it, and they had to jump a four-foot-high fence to get away from him! That memory could still make Lisa's heart skip a beat.

"Sure," Lisa said, trying to shift the topic. "And remember the time we had to ride like crazy to get away from a forest fire?"

"A forest fire?" Alice asked. She looked around at the woods and didn't see any sign of damage.

"It wasn't here," Lisa explained. "We were on a pack trip in the Rockies."

"It must have been scary," said Alice.

"It was. Especially when we had to jump our Western-trained horses over a fallen tree. Western saddles were definitely not made for jumping. Not like these, I mean."

"I wouldn't know," Alice said.

From Alice's tone of voice Lisa could tell that Alice wasn't interested in hearing more about jumping and how wonderful it was. But Lisa hoped that would all change after her first successful experience, which would occur in just a few minutes. They were nearing the spot on the trail where they'd left the tree trunk.

"Let's trot now," Stevie said.

"Is the ground smooth enough?" Alice asked.

"Oh, sure," Stevie said. "In fact, up ahead it gets even smoother and we can canter. Are you ready?"

"Definitely," Alice said. "I'm having a great time with you two. I just like to be on the safe side."

"I couldn't agree with you more," Stevie said as she signaled Topside to begin trotting.

"Trust us," Lisa said from behind. "You're safe with us all the way."

"I know," Alice said. "You're my kind of riders!"

The horses all began trotting then. Lisa held her breath. The tree was less than fifty yards away now. Stevie, in the lead, began cantering. That was the safest way to approach a jump. Starlight followed, just about twenty feet behind. Lisa, twenty feet behind Alice and Starlight, cantered as well.

Then, as Lisa knew it would, the path veered quite sharply to the left. They'd placed the jump about ten feet after the turn. Lisa listened carefully for the sound of Topside's jump, but couldn't hear it. She urged Barq forward then. She didn't want to miss Alice's jump.

The second Stevie landed, she drew Topside to the side of the trail and turned him around. She just had to see the look on Alice's face when she went over her first jump.

Starlight came around the bend at a rapid canter. He didn't even bat an eye when he spotted the tree trunk across the trail. He maintained his speed, and then just as if he'd been born to do it, he rose, pushing off with his strong rear legs and soaring over the obstacle.

Stevie couldn't contain her excitement.

"Wasn't that wonderful?" she asked, riding over to where Alice had drawn Starlight to a halt. "You did it perfectly. We knew you would. You're a natural jumper!"

Barq and Lisa completed the jump then and drew up beside Alice and Stevie.

"Wasn't it great?" Lisa asked. "Jumps in a ring are fine, but the best ones are the natural obstacles. Starlight knew just what to do, didn't he?"

Alice hadn't said anything, and that became the first indication to Lisa that maybe something was wrong.

"Are you all right?" Lisa asked.

"Of course she's all right," Stevie said, dismissing the question. "She jumped like the champion we knew she would be. She's not just all right. She's wonderful."

"You planned this?" Alice asked the girls.

"Sure did," Stevie said proudly. "And it worked, didn't it? Now you have a whole new thing to learn about riding. Not that there's much to learn, considering how well you went over your first jump!"

"You intentionally put that log where I wouldn't see it and where Starlight would just go over it?"

"It took a while to find the right place," Stevie said. "But we obviously picked the perfect one, right?"

"Perfect for what?" Alice said. There was a sharpness in her voice that finally alerted even Stevie to the fact that something was definitely wrong.

"Perfect to show you that jumping is wonderful and you have all the skills you need to do it very well," Stevie answered her. She was feeling a little defensive and hurt by the fact that Alice didn't seem to appreciate all the work she and Lisa had gone to to make this be just right.

"And who asked you to do it and said it would be okay?" Alice demanded. "Max Regnery wasn't behind this, was he?"

"No," Lisa said. "Max didn't know anything about it. It was our idea. We thought it was a good one."

"You thought wrong," Alice said.

Then, without a word, she turned Starlight around and began walking him back to Pine Hollow. She had him step back over the tree trunk very carefully.

"Alice?" Lisa called.

"Leave me alone."

"We just want to help," said Stevie.

"Then leave me alone from now on," retorted Alice. That was the last word she said to them. She never turned around again as she and Starlight made their way back.

"Shouldn't we go with her?" Lisa asked Stevie. She was concerned about Alice.

"What for?" Stevie said. "You heard her say she doesn't want to talk to us or be with us. We have to move the tree trunk off the trail now anyway."

"Won't she get lost?"

"Starlight knows the way. He'll get her back to the stable."

"Won't Max be angry with us for letting her ride back alone?" Lisa asked.

"So what else is new? He'd be angrier if he knew we'd lied about clearing the path," Stevie said.

The girls dismounted and secured their horses to a tree branch while they went to work moving the tree trunk a final time.

When the tree trunk was safely off the trail and into the woods, Lisa sat down on it, put her elbows on her knees and her chin in her hands.

"I don't understand," she said. "We were just trying to help. Why is Alice so angry with us?"

"I've been thinking about it, and I've decided that she's probably not all that angry," Stevie said. "It's just that we surprised her. Maybe she's really angry with herself for letting so many jumping opportunities go by without trying it before now. The way I figure it, by the time she gets back to Pine Hollow, she'll be really glad we tricked her and ashamed that she rode off alone."

"Maybe," said Lisa.

"Why, I bet she's waiting for us so that she can apologize," Stevie went on. "She's probably talked to Mrs. Reg and signed up for a zillion jump classes for the rest of the time she's here."

"Maybe," said Lisa.

But that wasn't the case. By the time they returned to Pine Hollow, there was no sign of Alice. The only indication that she'd been there at all was the fact that Starlight was standing in the paddock, tacked up and riderless.

WITHOUT A WORD Stevie and Lisa began doing the work they knew they had to do. First, they took care of the horses they'd been riding, untacking and grooming Topside and Barq. Then, when that was done and they'd each brought fresh hay and water to the horses, the girls met in Starlight's stall to take care of him. That was when Mrs. Reg appeared.

Mrs. Reg was Max's mother, and she was a friendly person, kind and motherly. She was well-known for her habit of keeping young riders busy with chores that needed to be done around the stable and for her endless supply of stories. Whenever something happened, Mrs. Reg told a story that didn't seem the least bit relevant to the circumstances. It usually took the girls a while to figure out what the point was, but when they did, they almost always learned something.

This time Mrs. Reg didn't have a chore, nor did she have a story. But she certainly had a piece of her mind to give to Stevie and Lisa.

"I saw that horse in his stall, all lathered up, with his tack on," she accused. "I don't know what you two think you were doing, but you didn't do it right. Alice Jackson came through here in a storm, just leaving Starlight alone. You two were responsible for her since she's a new rider here, and it was your job to see to it that she took proper care of your friend's horse."

"But Mrs. Reg—" Stevie began.

"No buts. You know the rules."

"We did take care of him," Lisa protested.

"After he'd been standing in his stall for a full half hour," Mrs. Reg said.

This didn't seem fair to Stevie. After all, they weren't responsible for the fact that Alice had ridden off in a huff. Nor could they help the fact that they had to stay in the woods to clear the path.

"But we—"

"No excuses," said Mrs. Reg. With that, she turned on her heel and marched back to her office, leaving the girls even more befuddled.

67

"That wasn't fair," said Stevie.

"Well, we couldn't tell her what we were doing in the woods, could we? We'd already told Max that we cleared the trail. It's a good thing she didn't know we lied to him. Then she'd *really* be angry."

"Well, we were that lucky, but it still wasn't fair that Alice left Starlight alone and left us to take the rap for it. She knows better than to leave a lathered horse tacked up in his stall."

"Maybe she didn't even cool him down," said Lisa. "Is he going to stiffen up? Should I walk him now?"

Stevie considered that for a few seconds. "No, I don't think so. Whatever he was when she put him in the stall, he's cooled down now. I don't think a walk will do him any good."

Lisa didn't like the idea that Starlight hadn't been perfectly taken care of while he was in their care. They'd made Carole a promise, and she felt as if they'd broken it.

"That ungrateful girl!" Stevie scowled. "First of all, she doesn't appreciate all the work we're doing for her, and then she goes and gets us into trouble with Mrs. Reg!"

"To say nothing of the fact that she might have hurt Starlight!" Lisa added.

"Yeah," Stevie agreed. "Poor Starlight." She turned

to the horse and looked at him. He didn't seem particularly troubled by anything. He seemed much more concerned with the mouthful of hay he was munching than with their problems. Stevie put her arms around his neck and gave him a hug. He kept right on munching.

"You know, I'd like to give Alice a piece of my mind!" said Stevie.

"That's a good idea," said Lisa. "If she expects to ride here again, she's going to have to prove she can take better care of the horses. And I think we should tell her that we can't trust her with Starlight again, so she'll have to ride one of Max's horses. I know that's not much of a threat, because all of Max's horses are great horses, but not very many of them are as good as Starlight!"

The anger felt good. At first the girls had just been confused by Alice's behavior and weren't sure how to react. But now, since Mrs. Reg had gotten angry at them for what Alice failed to do, they felt really mad.

"Let's go, then. Max isn't here. We can use the phone in his office," said Stevie.

"But we're not supposed to use the Pine Hollow phone unless it's a stable emergency," said Lisa. There was a pay phone the riders were expected to use for routine calls.

"This *is* a stable emergency," said Stevie. "Alice has to learn better, or some other horse will be hurt."

Lisa couldn't really disagree with that, so the two girls marched into Max's empty office.

It took Stevie just a few minutes to get Alice's grandmother's telephone number from the directory, and soon they had her on the phone.

"Is Alice there, please?" said Stevie.

The woman asked Stevie to wait while she called Alice to the phone. Stevie waited, but not patiently. As she waited, she could feel herself getting angrier and angrier. She remembered Alice's cold farewell and the danger she'd caused for Starlight. She remembered how hard she and Lisa had tried to make the ride very special for Alice. She remembered how she and Lisa had expected Alice to be thrilled.

"I don't know who it is," Stevie heard Alice's grandmother say.

There was a long silence.

"Come on, dear. They won't wait all day."

There was more silence. Then a tentative "Hello?"

"Alice? This is Stevie Lake," Stevie began. Then she continued without pause. She didn't want Alice to have a minute to get a word in until she'd said everything that was on her mind. Stevie told her how Mrs. Reg had gotten angry and how it wasn't fair to

70

Starlight, to say nothing of how it wasn't fair to her and to Lisa for Alice to treat a wonderful horse like Starlight in such an irresponsible manner and how horses needed to be cooled down and then untacked, fed, and watered, and how Alice knew perfectly well that all the riders at Pine Hollow were responsible for taking care of the horses they rode.

"And," Stevie concluded, "we thought you were a good rider, but we've learned that you're not, because no good rider would ever do that to a horse!"

Stevie had said all she'd wanted to say. Now it was Alice's turn. And when Alice finally spoke, it wasn't the humble apology that Stevie expected.

"It's not a question of whether I'm a good rider or not, Stevie," Alice said. "It's a question of whether I'm a rider or not. And I'm not. I quit. Good-bye."

She hung up the phone.

"What did she say?" Lisa asked, looking with concern at a very rare sight—a speechless Stevie Lake.

"She said she's never going to ride a horse again," Stevie said. "And I think she means it."

8

"THERE'S A STRANGE elbow sticking into me," Sheila announced.

"Not all *that* strange," said Carole. "It's mine." Carole tried to shift her position in the backseat of Uncle Willie's car so she wasn't poking Sheila, but then she found she was crushing Aunt Joanna, who then squished Colonel Hanson. All four of them were in the back because Uncle Willie and Midge Ford were in the front bucket seats.

The group was headed for Disney World, and Carole was very excited about it. She and Sheila had been up late the night before, reading a guidebook and trying to decide what they were going to do first.

Since Sheila lived nearby, she'd been to the theme parks many times, but it was all still very exciting to her, and she was looking forward to showing it to her younger cousin.

Carole flipped open the guidebook and looked once again.

"What about this Tea Party thing?" she asked.

"That's for little kids," Sheila said.

"But it looks like fun," said Carole.

"It is," Sheila conceded. "We have to do it. We'll just pretend we're little kids."

That seemed to Carole like a good attitude for a whole day at the Magic Kingdom.

"My first stop is the Big Thunder Mountain Railroad," Colonel Hanson declared. "Are you game for that, Midge?"

"In your dreams! That's a roller coaster!"

"I know," said Carole's father. "And I just love roller coasters."

"Wait until you try Space Mountain," said Aunt Joanna. "That might change your mind. It's a roller coaster completely in the dark."

"It's supposed to be really scary, Uncle Mitch," Sheila said. "I remember one time I went on that when my class had a day outing at the park. Colin McKenzie—"

"Ahem," Uncle Willie interrupted.

"Enough," said Aunt Joanna.

Naturally, that made Carole very curious. "What?" she whispered to Sheila.

"Threw up!" Sheila whispered back, but she whispered it loud enough so that everybody could hear. That made Colonel Hanson laugh, and when Colonel Hanson laughed, everybody around him laughed, too. In fact, all six people in the car were laughing by the time they reached the parking lot.

Once they got inside the park and were oriented, they agreed to break up into what Carole's father called "interest groups." The "interest group" that was headed for the terrifying rides, Space Mountain and Big Thunder Mountain, included Carole and her father. Aunt Joanna and Uncle Willie wanted to go on the Skyway—a funicular that reached from Tomorrowland to Fantasyland. Sheila decided she couldn't wait to see the Mad Tea Party, and Midge felt the same way. Their interest group was headed there.

Then Colonel Hanson announced that they should all meet at one of the restaurants at noon—it took only fifteen minutes to argue about which one—to eat lunch and rearrange their interest groups. Carole liked the fact that her father, who was in the military, was a natural-born leader and made good decisions. This was definitely going to be fun.

Colonel Hanson offered his arm to his daughter, and the two of them headed for Frontierland and their first roller coaster of the day.

There was a lot to see on the way to Frontierland. First of all, there were the sights that had been planned by the builders of the place—the castle that was at the center of it all, the play areas of Tom Sawyer's Island, and people enjoying Mike Fink's River Boats. There was a shooting gallery, where they stopped briefly.

"Are you a crack shot, Dad?" Carole asked, remembering that her father had gotten several medals for his shooting ability in the Marine Corps.

"The country is safe with me," he assured her. Then he put some change on the counter and picked up a rifle. While Carole watched, holding her breath in preparation of being awed by her father's skill, he took aim. Slowly, smoothly, he squeezed the trigger.

"Ping!" The shot fired. Then nothing.

The Colonel looked puzzled.

"I think you missed, Dad. Try again."

"Missed? No way," he declared. But he prepared to try again. Another *ping*, another miss. He had ten shots. Finally, on the seventh shot, he hit something, a light blinked, a bell sounded.

"Nice shootin' there, pardner," said the young man behind the counter.

Two more misses.

"Well, I suggest you steer away from a career as a sharpshooter," the man said.

Colonel Hanson just gave him a dirty look.

Carole wanted to try. She picked up a gun and took aim. It didn't seem so hard. She just lined up the two little markers on the barrel with a target and—

Ping! Ding! Flash!

"Good!" said the young man.

It really was easy. In ten shots Carole got seven hits.

"You should give your father some pointers," the young man said as they walked away.

"You *were* trying to miss, weren't you, Dad?" Carole asked.

"Well, it's very different using that kind of simple rifle," he said, obviously ducking her question. "In the Marine Corps, we're expected to know how to manage a complicated piece of equipment. Our weapons are high tech, and—"

"You mean you *weren't* trying to miss?" she teased.

"I think it's this way to Big Thunder Mountain," he said.

There was a short line at Big Thunder Mountain. They waited only a few minutes before boarding the "mining cars" of the roller coaster to begin a wonderful and exciting ride. As the little car jerked up and around, down and under, through the course of the ride, Carole and her father gripped the handrail with an iron-tight grasp. They cried, Oooh! Aaaaahhhh! and *Yeoooooooow!* together. And when they got off, neither would admit to the other that they'd been scared. Carole just gave her father a big hug. Then, when they saw that there was almost no line, they went right back in and did it again.

That left them enough time to go on Space Mountain twice before it was time to meet the rest of the family for lunch. If Big Thunder Mountain was scary, Space Mountain was terrifying, and both Carole and her father adored every second of it!

As they headed for the meeting place, they took a brief detour to Mars and ate ice-cream bars in the shape of a certain familiar mouse. Even though they arrived at the restaurant two minutes late (it was actually ninety seconds according to Colonel Hanson's watch), they were the first ones to get there. Everybody else was obviously having a good time, too.

Once all six of them were at the restaurant, they began swapping tales of their adventures. Sheila couldn't stop talking about the Pirates of the Caribbean. Colonel Hanson said he had to see that next. Aunt Joanna agreed and asked Midge if she'd like to come along with them. Midge said she'd been on the Pirates with Sheila, but wanted to buy a present for her son. Carole wanted to buy some things for Lisa and Stevie, so she said she'd go shopping with Midge. Uncle Willie said *he* wanted to try Space Mountain. Carole had loved it, but twice was enough. Sheila thought that, in spite of Colin McKenzie's experience, she'd like to do that with her father. Thus, a whole new set of "interest groups" was born, though Carole could see that Aunt Joanna was disappointed about something. When they'd all finished eating, they agreed on their next meeting time and place. It would be on Main Street in time for the parade.

Midge and Carole set off together and began poking into the zillions of specialty shops that seemed to be everywhere.

"What was the matter with Aunt Joanna?" Carole asked Midge.

"I think I let her down," Midge answered.

"How's that?"

"Well, to be honest with you, she thinks I ought to

be sticking closer to your father. She said as much to me before we got to the table at the restaurant."

"Oh. That's right. She's trying to fix you up with Dad, isn't she?"

Carole was embarrassed to have said it, even though she knew it was true. Midge laughed at her bluntness.

"Yes, she is," Midge said.

"But you don't want to be fixed up? You don't like Dad?" Carole surprised herself with the bold question. She couldn't understand how any sensible woman wouldn't be in love with her father, who was without a doubt the most wonderful guy in the world.

"Of course I like your dad," Midge said. "He's a great guy. He's kind, he's funny, and he's warm. Your dad isn't the problem."

"Then what is?" Carole asked.

Midge paused at a cart that sold popcorn and soda. She bought a bag of popcorn and a soda for each of them. Then they sat down on a nearby bench and rested their feet while they talked.

"There are two problems, Carole," Midge began. "The first is that I've been divorced for just a short time. It's been a very difficult time for me and hard on my son as well. Something like this makes wounds.

79

The wounds heal in time, but right now they're still not healed and they hurt."

"You mean you're not ready to see anybody yet?" she asked.

"I'm ready to see people. I'm just not ready to get serious about anybody or anything. That's going to take a long time."

"I can understand that. You mean you like being with my dad, but you couldn't fall in love with anybody right now?"

Midge nodded.

"Okay, so what's the other problem?"

"The other problem is your aunt Joanna. She's a meddler. She thinks she knows what's right for me and she thinks she knows what's right for your dad. I think she's wrong on both counts, but she's a good friend of mine and I love her a lot. I don't want to hurt her feelings, but I'm not going to pretend something just to make her feel good. Besides that, if your father and I *were* to start seeing one another—a tricky business considering how far apart we live—Joanna would never be able to keep her fingers out of it. She'd be telling him things about me constantly and she'd be telling me things about him all the time. She'd want to run the whole thing. Why, I'm telling you, Carole, I swear that somewhere in the back of her mind are wedding plans for us. She asked me what size dress I wore, and I'll bet you she's got her own wedding dress in the attic and that's what she's thinking!"

Carole started laughing and found herself choking on some popcorn. Midge waited patiently until she recovered.

"What was that all about?" she asked.

Carole took a sip of her soda. "Well, Midge, if she's got a wedding dress in her attic, she may also have some bridesmaid's dresses, too, because she was asking me what size dress *I* wore."

Midge laughed then, too. "And what did you tell her?"

"I told her I don't wear dresses. I'm usually in jeans or riding clothes. That made her scowl."

Carole thought for a minute then. "I suppose that if you and Dad each reminded Aunt Joanna that you've been doing fine on your own for some time now and don't really need her help, she just wouldn't believe you, would she?"

"I considered it," Midge said. "But you're right. Either she wouldn't believe me or else she'd be hurt. Besides, someday I may be ready to fall for a guy she says is perfect for me. Someday that might be your dad. Not today, though. Incidentally, I have the feeling that he feels about the same way. He's talked an awful lot about another woman, one named Dana? I think he's more than a little sweet on her, and I think she's a very lucky woman."

"I think so, too," said Carole. She wouldn't have minded telling Midge more about Mrs. Dana, but she thought it was her father's job to do that. She didn't want to meddle. One meddler in the family was enough.

"Now don't we have some shopping to do?" Midge asked.

They did, indeed. In the next hour and a half, Carole thought they went into forty shops, and she also thought they'd left another forty untouched. She'd intended to buy only little gifts for Stevie and Lisa, but found that there was so much to buy that, well, she couldn't help herself. She stopped only when she ran out of money. By then, it was time for the parade.

While they waited for the parade to begin, Carole scribbled a postcard to Lisa and Stevie. She wrote, "This place is fantastic. And tomorrow may be even better. I'm going riding on the beach with Sheila. Can't wait. And can't wait to see you! Love, Carole."

The rest of the day was as magical as the start had been. The parade featured lots of familiar characters, bright lights, grand music, marching bands, and circus-style performers. There was time after the parade for them to have another set of "interest groups," and that took Carole and Sheila to the Mad Tea Party as well as the Haunted House, the Jungle Cruise, and into a submarine that took them Twenty Thousand Leagues Under the Sea. The girls were totally exhausted by the time they met up with the rest of the group, but a good dinner woke them up enough so that they could stay alert for the fireworks spectacle. After all, who could sleep through fireworks?

Completely spent, the six weary fun seekers made their way back to Uncle Willie's car. Nobody complained about poking elbows on the way back. Everybody but Uncle Willie, who was driving, was too sound asleep.

9

When Carole woke up the next morning, she knew there was something special coming. She just couldn't remember what it was. The sun shone brightly through the window of Sheila's room. That was a hint, she knew. In the kitchen downstairs, she heard somebody drop something. It made a nice comfortable thumping sound—just like the sound of a hoofbeat. That was it. She and Sheila were going to have a horseback picnic on the beach. That was more than enough to make any day special!

She sat up and climbed out of bed.

"Come on, let's get going," she said to Sheila in the bed next to hers. But Sheila wasn't there. Carole glanced at her watch. It was nine-fifteen already. Sheila was probably the one who'd dropped something in the kitchen and Carole should be down there, too, helping to make their picnic.

Carole washed and dressed quickly and then went down the back stairs.

Sheila and Aunt Joanna were in the kitchen, and they were both working. They were also talking, and Carole had the feeling an interruption right then might not be welcome.

"I'm telling you, Sheila, you're going to have to get rid of that pony. He's just eating up a lot of hay and doing you no good at all."

"But Mom, that's *Maverick* you're talking about," Sheila said. "He's like my best friend."

"He's no friend to you when he's keeping you from winning any ribbons in every show you enter. You're a full-sized rider and you need a full-sized horse.

As Carole listened, she could tell that these words had been well rehearsed by both Joanna and Sheila. It was a tired argument and it was going nowhere. Carole took another step down the stairs to put an end to the argument, at least temporarily, when it took another turn.

"Look at your cousin Carole," Aunt Joanna persisted. "She's got a new horse—practically a green horse—and she's trained it so well that she got the reserve champion ribbon in the junior intermediate division at Briarwood! And she's younger than you are!"

Carole was uncomfortable with that. Even though Aunt Joanna was right, she *had* gotten the reserve champion ribbon, she didn't like the fact that she was being used for comparison in a disagreement between Joanna and Sheila. Sheila was bound to be resentful and Carole was embarrassed and a little bit annoyed to find herself part of this ongoing fight.

"Carole is a very good rider," Sheila said. Carole sighed with relief. At least Sheila wasn't openly resentful. "And she's put in hours and hours of work training that horse."

"You could do the same," said Aunt Joanna.

"And I'd be glad to do it—with somebody else's horse."

"Good morning!" Carole said cheerfully.

"Oh, hi, we were just talking about you," Aunt Joanna said. "I was telling Sheila how proud your dad was about the reserve champion ribbon you won at Briarwood with that new horse of yours, Starlight."

"That was a fun experience," Carole said. "But I have the feeling that our picnic on the beach is going to be even more fun. What do you know about the horse I'm riding?"

"He's a great chestnut gelding named Brandy," Sheila began. And she had a lot more to say about him than that. Carole sighed with relief as she listened to a description of Brandy's wonderful qualities. She'd managed to shift the topic of conversation. The only other time the issue arose before they left for their picnic was when Aunt Joanna and Carole were alone.

"You've just got to talk her into letting us sell that old pony!" Aunt Joanna said. "He's not doing her any good at all, and she simply refuses to consider it. She's so stubborn! It comes from her father's side of the family, you know—"

At that Carole stifled a laugh. Sheila's stubbornness absolutely did not come from Uncle Willie! Luckily Sheila joined them before Carole could respond.

"Ready?" Sheila asked.

"You bet!" Carole said, and she meant it.

An hour later Carole was mounted on Brandy and fully informed about him. She had been told that he had a sweet disposition and tended to be a little lazy, but he was extremely gentle and would try to please her, as long as she didn't use the crop on him in front of the girth. He would spook if she did that. Since it wasn't considered proper form to use the crop any-place but on a horse's rear, Carole was sure she and Brandy wouldn't have any trouble.

Sheila was mounted on Maverick. He was a pretty pony with a sleek coat and bright eyes. His ears flicked alertly, and he seemed ready to do whatever Sheila asked of him. There was a closeness between them that Carole had seen only rarely between horse and rider. Sheila gave Maverick near invisible instructions with the slightest pressure of her legs, and he re-sponded instantly. Clearly this pair had done so much together for so long that they understood each other perfectly.

It was true that Sheila looked a little odd on the pony. Maverick wasn't in any danger with a full-sized person in his saddle, but the proportion of rider to horse was definitely wrong.

Carole rode Brandy around the stable's ring a few times to get the feel of him and to let him do the same of her. It didn't take long for each to know that the other was a natural. Carole walked, trotted, and can-tered and then slowed the gaits until they were walk-ing again.

"We're ready," she announced, and the stable owner agreed.

Sheila opened the gates of the ring, and the two of them rode out.

The path led from the ring down to the seaside. Carole was accustomed to seeing fields and woods beyond the riding ring, not palm trees and sand. It was beautiful! And then there was the ocean, the Atlantic. Down here in Florida it wasn't the musty gray that it was on the northern coasts. It was a startling aqua blue.

The horses stepped on the sand tentatively at first, and then, as they neared the water and the sand became firmer, the horses were more sure-footed.

They walked for a while, allowing both the horses and riders to become accustomed to the seashore. For Carole, it was somewhat a matter of getting used to the feel of a horse who was walking on sand, but it was more a matter of taking in the sights.

"This is great!" she declared.

"Sure is," Sheila agreed.

To their right was what seemed like an endless line of palm trees, shading the upper reaches of the beach. Some had coconuts and some just long, broad leaves that moved gently in the sea breeze, shifting the shadows along the edge of the beach.

To their left was an endless expanse of aqua water, dotted here and there by boats, small sailboats, large sailboats, powerboats and ocean liners. There were also a few tankers and barges, but those were farther away. They reminded Carole that the ocean wasn't just for pleasure. It served as a major conduit of transportation and commerce for the entire coastal area.

A speedboat zipped along nearby, skipping across the waves, from crest to crest. It made a horrendous noise, and Brandy flinched ever so slightly. Carole shortened the reins and held a little more tightly with her legs. The horse was reassured by her strength, and relaxed.

"Ready to try trotting?" Sheila asked.

Carole was ready and said so. Maverick started his easy, smooth trot, and it took little work to convince Brandy to follow suit. Carole rose and sat with the beat of his gait, posting naturally. She always enjoyed trotting, and Brandy seemed to agree that it was a nice way to go. Although Carole had been warned that Brandy could be lazy, he kept his gait and didn't give Carole a minute of concern.

"Canter?"

"Yes!" Carole called back to her cousin.

Brandy heard the word and was ready. The instant Maverick began cantering, Brandy began as well.

Brandy was a full-sized horse, and though Maverick had quick gaits for a pony, he was just a pony, and his legs were shorter than Brandy's. Within a few strides, Brandy was ready to pass Maverick. Carole held Brandy back. Sheila was in the lead and should stay that way. Brandy obeyed, though Carole thought she could sense his disappointment. He shortened his stride and remained in place behind Maverick.

Cantering on Brandy was just as much fun as trotting. The palm trees to their right seemed to whiz by them. A few swimmers and sunbathers stood up from their towels to watch the girls ride by. Some waved. Carole waved back. It was almost like being in a parade!

Sheila drew Maverick back down to a walk.

"Dad was going to drop off our picnic up here a bit," she said. She rose in the saddle to see if she could spot her father. There was Uncle Willie, standing in the shade of a palm tree, next to a large picnic cooler and some buckets for the horses. He was waving at his daughter.

At first the girls had wanted to carry the picnic themselves, but when Aunt Joanna kept adding goodies for them to eat and drink, it became apparent that they were going to have trouble carrying all that on their horses. Then, when Sheila and Carole began adding things of their own, suntan lotion, towels, snorkels and masks, flutterboards, they just had to ask

Uncle Willie to help. He was glad to do so, and the girls suspected that was, in part, because it would allow him to give them one more warning about being careful.

"Now watch out for the surf," he said as they approached him at a walk. "There are other swimmers around today, but I don't see a lifeguard. . . ." He pointed to the empty tower nearby.

"She's probably just on her lunch break," Sheila said.

"I hope so," said Uncle Willie. "And don't go in swimming right after you eat, and—"

"All right, all right," said Sheila. "We know what we're doing. Trust us."

Uncle Willie smiled. "It's just because I love you, you know."

"I know," Sheila said. And she gave him a hug. "We'll see you in a couple of hours. We'll wait for you to pick this stuff up before we ride back, okay?"

"Deal," he said. But then he lingered.

"Good-bye," Sheila said pointedly. He waved and then left.

Sheila and Carole untacked the horses and put lead ropes on their halters so they could be secured to a palm tree in the shade. Carole took the two buckets Uncle Willie had brought and filled them with water

92

from the nearby freshwater fountain. The horses seemed grateful for the drink after the brisk ride on the beach. Carole refilled the buckets and left them where the horses could reach them if they needed more.

While Carole took care of the horses, Sheila took care of herself and Carole. By the time Carole was done, Sheila had stripped down to her bathing suit and laid out a fabulous spread for their picnic. Aunt Joanna had managed to put in some things that they hadn't even known about.

"Deviled eggs!" Sheila declared.

"And look at those fresh veggies," said Carole, taking off her riding clothes as well. The warm sun felt wonderful.

The deviled eggs and fresh vegetables were just the appetizers. There was cold fried chicken, potato salad, and lots of juice. There were choices of fruit, brownies, and chocolate-chip cookies for dessert. Carole and Sheila couldn't decide which of those they liked the best, so they did the only logical thing and ate them all.

They gave a few of the leftover vegetables and fruits to the horses, who seemed particularly grateful for the carrots and apples, but munched the green peppers as well.

The last item in the cooler was a box of after-dinner mints!

"Your mother doesn't miss anything, does she?" Carole asked, taking one of the mints.

"She can be totally annoying," Sheila said, and Carole didn't have to ask what she meant. "But she's also kind, generous, and thoughtful, and a wonderful mother."

"Those are traits that run in the family," Carole said, reaching for another mint and thinking of Aunt Joanna's brother, her own father.

"Yeah," Sheila agreed.

Carole and Sheila each lay on the blanket, propping themselves up with their elbows and looking out at the ocean and the boats and ships that seemed to move so slowly on its surface. Behind them, in the shade, the horses rested, snorting contentedly every once in a while. Nearby, a few fellow picnickers finished their meals, dabbled in the water, and worked on sand castles.

Carole eased her feet under a layer of silky white sand. It was hard to believe that just about a thousand miles away, her friends were wearing sweaters, maybe jackets, and here on the Florida beach, Carole was considering getting into the water to cool off. It was too soon after lunch, however. She'd just have to rest a little bit before swimming. She lowered herself so she lay flat, put her hat over her face, and closed her eyes. She sighed with contentment. After all, what could be more perfect than perfect weather on a perfect beach after a perfect meal and a perfect horseback ride?

She slept.

"COME ON, SURF'S up," Sheila said, nudging Carole awake. Carole looked at her watch. She'd been napping for half an hour. That should be long enough for the delicious lunch to settle down. It was time to play in the water.

She stood up and dusted the sand off her. She looked around. The horses were still safely in the shade. Nearby, picnickers were packing up the remains of their lunches and heading back home, so she and Sheila were the only ones in the area. Carole liked that. It helped her to pretend that she and Sheila were surviving alone together on this beautiful beach with only the water to play in and only the horses to ride.

Sheila took her hand. "Come on, sleepyhead," she said. "Let's go!"

They ran down to the water's edge. The aqua waves were breaking about thirty yards from shore. By the time the water reached the beach, it was just a gentle white foam that licked at the girls' toes while they stood tentatively, waiting for the right moment to enter.

"It's so warm!" Carole declared. Every time she'd swum in the ocean, it had been quite chilly, but that wasn't the case here. It was warm, welcoming, and velvety smooth. She waded out confidently. Sheila was right by her side.

The water remained very shallow, knee-deep, for quite a while, and then it dropped suddenly to waist-deep. From there, it progressed. The girls walked out until they thought it was about shoulder-deep, but they couldn't tell for sure because the water never stayed one depth long enough for them to measure. They were near where the waves were breaking, and Carole could feel the powerful surge of the ocean water. It was something.

"Never turn your back on the ocean!" Sheila said, and she said it just in time, too, because when Carole looked over her shoulder, all she could see was an enormous wave that seemed about to swallow her.

"Jump!" Sheila called out.

Carole jumped. She rose about two feet from her own strength and another five with the power of the wave. The surf picked her up, lifted her high, brought her toward the beach, and then set her down gently. She had time only to take a nice deep breath before the returning water began pushing her back, carrying her toward the next incoming wave.

It was like Space Mountain, Big Thunder Mountain, and the Mad Tea Party all rolled into one, only there was no waiting time, because right away another wave was coming. Carole jumped the next wave and then watched Sheila bodysurf toward shore.

"That looks like fun," she called to her cousin.

"It is!" Sheila replied, and then gave Carole a few tips on how to do it. When Carole was ready to give it a try, Sheila pointed out a good wave.

Carole faced the beach and felt the powerful push-pull of the ocean behind her. She looked over her shoulder at the coming wave.

"Now!" Sheila yelled.

Carole pushed off from the bottom, rising high into the curl of the wave. She could feel the swell of water pushing her upward and toward the shore. She put her arms out straight in front of herself and pointed her toes as Sheila had instructed, thinking that the more she resembled a surfboard, the better off she'd be.

The wave propelled her forward at an incredible speed. She was completely surrounded by it and trapped in its power, rushing toward the shore. Then, just as she began to slow down, the crest of the wave caught up with her, folded itself over her, and wrapped itself around her. At the last possible second, Carole remembered one more piece of Sheila's advice and took a deep breath. The wave came crashing down on her, pulled her deeper into the water, and drew her back away from the shore. A second later she felt herself pop up to the surface. She lifted her head, cleared her eyes of the salt water, and began laughing.

It was almost as much fun as horseback riding!

"Isn't it fabulous?" Sheila asked.

"Absolutely," agreed Carole. "As long as you don't mind getting sand in everything."

Sheila laughed. "It's a small price to pay for something that's this much fun. It's even better with a flutterboard—wait here while I go get it. Don't do any surfing without me. I'll be right back."

Carole didn't mind waiting. She played in the

waves, jumping over them and diving into them until Sheila could get back with the board. Sheila had to go quite a distance, too. Their picnic area seemed to have moved about fifty yards down the beach.

Carole swam outward toward the place where the waves began to crest. She wanted to be ready to use the flutterboard as soon as Sheila got back with it. A nice-sized wave came. Carole jumped up into it and enjoyed the frothy lathering she got as the crest passed her by. The wave had broken so quickly that she hadn't had time to take the breath she'd needed, and she found herself with a snootful of salt water. She coughed and tried to clear out her nose. Then she rubbed at her eyes, now tearing because of the salty water.

She was so busy with the problems the last wave had caused, she never saw the next wave when it came. Only instinct caused her to take a deep breath when it hit.

In an instant Carole was completely submerged in the surf. This time, instead of propelling her upward and toward the shore, it pulled her down, tugging fiercely at her feet, dragging her down to the sandy bottom.

Carole had never felt a force like this. There was no fighting it. It was mightier than a team of horses, stronger than anything she'd ever known. Her hair swarmed around her, tugged every which way by the water. Her body scraped the bottom, and where the sand had once seemed silky, it now abraded her skin. And her lungs screamed for air.

Carole didn't know how far she traveled or how long she stayed underwater, but when the water above her lightened, she knew she was near the surface and could finally use her arms to help. She struggled, swimming and fighting against the powerful force. She kicked, remembering her own horse's powerful legs as he flew over the highest jumps.

"Up, Starlight, up!" she urged herself. And then she popped to the surface and gasped, coughing and sputtering.

At first she was so relieved to be breathing that she didn't realize she still seemed to have no control over her destiny. She was out beyond the line where the waves broke, and she was being pulled farther away from the shore at every second. She could breathe all right, but she could feel the water pulling at her feet, as if it felt cheated and wanted to swallow her up again. The next time it might be for good. Carole was too exhausted to win another battle against the ocean.

Sheila. Where was Sheila?

Carole squinted. Her cousin had just picked up the flutterboard and was returning to the ocean. Carole waved for help.

Sheila waved back.

Carole cried for help.

Sheila waved, obviously completely unaware that Carole was in trouble.

"Help!"

Sheila held up the flutterboard to show that she had it.

Carole wasn't going to get help from Sheila. What could her cousin do, anyway? If she came out into this water, then the two of them might be killed.

Carole tried swimming. It took all her might to get her feet up out of the deep water and begin kicking. She moved her arms. Carole was a good swimmer. She'd been swimming all her life. But she'd never been swimming like this. With each stroke it was harder to lift her arms and kick her feet. With each stroke she was farther from shore.

Sheila waded into the water and looked at Carole again. Then she saw what was happening. Carole wasn't playing in the waves. Carole was in a riptide, and she was being carried out into the ocean—out where the liners and gas tankers were, out where there was nothing but water and danger and, for swimmers

—she didn't even want to think about it. This was trouble. Big time.

"Help!" Sheila cried. The nearby picnickers had gone, and the lifeguard tower was still empty. They were alone and Carole was in great danger.

Sheila looked around desperately. All she saw was the peaceful beach where they'd had their picnic and where their horses were now enjoying the shade of the coconut palm. Maverick looked up when she looked up at him. His ears flicked and his nostrils flared as if he understood there was danger.

Maverick, her beloved pony. He could help. He was the only possible answer.

Without a second's hesitation, Sheila dropped the flutterboard and ran to the palm tree. She unhitched the knot in Maverick's lead rope and leapt onto his back.

"Let's go, boy," she said. He went.

Carole continued to struggle against the water. Every inch of her body told her she must not allow herself to be dragged out into the ocean. She kicked, she used her arms, she kept moving, and she kept going farther out.

Suddenly there was a tug at her feet as the water seemed to suck her under again. She filled her lungs with air just before she went under. Again, she was relentlessly pulled by the force of the water, down and out she went. She was swirled around as if by water going down a drain. Then, as suddenly as she'd gone down, she popped up. She gasped for air and looked around. The beach was very far away now, the few figures mere dots on the pure white sand. There was one that was bigger, though.

Carole looked carefully. She couldn't see very well because of the glare, and she was becoming so tired that she couldn't hold her arm up to shade her eyes for more than a few seconds.

It wasn't a person she saw entering the water. It was more than a person; it was a horse, a horse she'd seen before, but she couldn't remember where. And the rider—she knew the rider. Definitely. But who was it? The water tugged again, then. Carole took another deep breath and prepared for another terrifying ride to the deep.

Maverick entered the water fearlessly, trotting straight into the powerful surf just as Sheila told him to do. He didn't flinch when the water was at his knees or splashing on his chest. Sheila gripped tightly and prepared for the onslaught as they approached the area where the surf might grab at them, too. She spoke to her pony with her legs and he answered with his heart and all his strength. Soon he was bounding into the surf, jumping up against the oncoming waves just as Sheila and Carole had been doing only a few minutes ago. This time, however, it wasn't for fun. It was for real.

Sheila sat up tall on the pony's back. Where was Carole? She shaded her eyes to look and, at first, couldn't see anything of her cousin.

She looked to the right where the undertow had carried them. Then she looked out. In the distance, perhaps a quarter of a mile away, Carole bobbed helplessly.

While Maverick moved forward toward Carole, Sheila considered the circumstances. She knew what was going on, but Carole did not. This was a riptide: an incredibly strong surface current that was pulling Carole down into the ocean and away from the shore. There was no way a single swimmer could defeat the force of the riptide. Fighting it would surely only lead to exhaustion, and exhaustion led to a place Sheila didn't want to think about.

The only way to defeat the riptide was to get out of its force. Since it could be a mile or more long, straight away from the beach, the only option was to move parallel to the beach, beyond the section affected by the riptide. Somehow Sheila had to convince Carole to stop swimming toward the beach and start swimming parallel to it.

Carole saw her then. She knew who that was. It was her cousin Sheila and Sheila was riding a horse. It was her horse. It was—she couldn't remember the horse's name. He had a name, she was sure, but she couldn't remember. She'd remember if only she could swim toward them. She wanted to reach them. She lifted one arm, put it in front of her, and kicked weakly. It wasn't an arm, though, really. It was some sort of very heavy attachment to her body. It just fell back into the water and hung limply by her side.

The girl was waving. The girl—Sheila—was waving. Carole wanted to wave back, but her arm weighed too much. Why did that girl want to wave? She wasn't waving hello. She was waving go away. Carole was going away. Far away. Carole began thinking about her mother then. She hadn't seen her in a long time. Something had happened to her, hadn't it? Carole struggled to remember. She missed her mother. Where was she? Was she far away? Carole didn't think so, but she couldn't remember. The water tugged at her feet again. It was cold, but so was she.

Sheila could tell that Carole didn't know what she wanted her to do. Carole just had to swim sideways. It was the only way—unless Maverick could get to her,

106

and then all three of them would go sideways together.

She shifted Maverick's direction then. They had to
go down the beach beyond where Carole was now.
They would have to be beyond the force of the riptide
and make Carole swim toward them. She hurried the
horse, who obeyed every command. When the water
got too deep for him to stand and walk, he simply
swam, strongly, bravely, and she rode on his back.

"Carole!" she called. "Swim to your left!" Carole
couldn't hear her.

With every stride, Maverick brought her closer to
Carole. Sheila didn't know what would happen if she
and Maverick got caught in the riptide, but she knew
what would happen if they didn't reach Carole, so
there didn't seem to be any choice. They persisted.
The pony never complained, never faltered. He
snorted to get the water out of his nose, and he swam
and swam and swam.

Suddenly Carole didn't feel any more pulling. The
torturous tugging stopped. She was vaguely aware of
the motion of the ocean around her, rocking, reassuring water everywhere. But no more tugging. Carole
rolled over on her back. She laid her head on the
water and looked up at the blue sky above. Her arms
rose and so did her legs. She closed her eyes. She was

very tired. She should sleep now, she thought. Yes, sleep.

Sheila saw Carole then. Her eyes were closed. She was floating on her back, rising and falling with the swell of the ocean. Sheila didn't know what was happening, but she knew that, one way or another, Carole was no longer being held by the riptide. It meant that it might be safe to swim near her now.

"Over there, boy," she told Maverick, and aimed the pony toward where Carole was.

"Carole! Are you okay? Carole!"

There was no answer. Then Carole lifted one hand just a little bit as if to wave to Sheila. It seemed a very odd gesture, but it was a gesture and assured Sheila that Carole was alive.

It took another few minutes for the pony and rider to reach Carole. Although Sheila and Maverick were both themselves exhausted by the swim, Sheila knew they had more reserve strength than Carole, who seemed barely aware of where she was.

Sheila checked her balance, leaned over, and grabbed one of Carole's arms.

"Come on up here, girl," Sheila said, trying to sound as if she knew exactly what she was doing.

"Wake me later," Carole said. "Later. I'll sleep now." She closed her eyes then, almost defiantly.

Sheila pulled. She pulled hard, drawing her cousin up out of the water. Carole was certainly not capable of sitting on Maverick on her own, and Sheila couldn't put Carole across the pony's back because she might fall off, and even if she didn't, her face would then be hanging in the water.

She finally got Carole onto the pony's back in front of her. Carole slumped forward. Sheila didn't know how well she'd stay there, but it was the best she could do. It was time to begin the long journey back to the beach.

Carole felt the pony's mane in her face. She didn't know what horse it was, but it was a nice horse. It smelled of the ocean, but it smelled of horse, too. That was a good smell.

"Nice horse," she mumbled. She closed her eyes. It was a good horse. It needed a hug. She'd been doing a lot of hugging lately. This creature seemed to need a hug more than anybody else. She hugged.

Sheila didn't know why it was that Carole was holding on so tight to Maverick's neck, but she knew that it was keeping Carole from falling off and into the ocean, so it was fine with her.

Maverick seemed to understand that he had to get back to shore. Sheila knew he couldn't have much energy left, nor did she. She didn't want to think what might happen if they didn't reach land soon.

One of the first rules of riding was that you should always look where you wanted your horse to go. On dry land a horse might misunderstand the slight changes in balance caused by a turned head and shift his own direction. Sheila didn't know if it was the same in the water, but that seemed logical. She stared at the shore ahead, now nearing. She was only barely aware of their progress as they rode and swam through the line of surf that now helped to carry them to safety. Maverick pushed himself up and rode on the force of the waves, grasping for footing each time the ocean set them back down again, each time a little closer to shore.

Sheila saw people gather there, people who hadn't been there before, people who had come to watch and people who had come to help. She thought she saw some men wading into the surf with life preservers and ropes. She thought she saw an ambulance. Then she thought she saw her father. And there was Uncle Mitch.

Maybe not. She was too tired now to be sure. She knew only that she and her pony and her cousin were going toward the shore. They were going to get there.

Maverick's feet struck sand. He was walking now,

110

not swimming. He struggled with the weight of the two girls on his back; he struggled with his own exhaustion. He took more steps. He paused. Without any signal from Sheila, he walked forward toward the beach, the dry sand, toward safety.

Sheila heard voices. She saw hands reaching for her and for Carole. She felt Maverick snort weakly and then stumble.

That was the last thing she remembered.

11

LISA PUT THE last breakfast dish in the dishwasher, rolled the racks in, and shut the door. Then she wiped the sink dry. It wasn't until she noticed that she was doing the wiping with her own shirttail that it occurred to her that her mind was not totally occupied with washing the breakfast dishes. A glance back in the dishwasher confirmed her suspicions. She'd put the tea kettle in there, too!

She rescued the tea kettle, put it back on the stove, turned out the kitchen light, and retreated to her room. It was school vacation for her, but it wasn't vacation for her parents. They'd both gone to work and she was alone in the house. She thought she might do some work on her science report that was due in three weeks, but try as she might to concentrate on electricity, all she could think about was Alice Jackson.

Lisa closed her book and climbed onto her bed. That was where she did her best thinking, especially if her dog, Dolly, joined her. She invited her up. Dolly was only too happy to oblige. The Lhasa apso jumped right onto the bed and settled herself onto Lisa's lap. Lisa patted her and thought. She found she could do those two things at the same time.

She and Stevie had only been trying to help Alice. Lisa certainly would be grateful to friends who tried to do that for her. She was sure Stevie and Carole would be, too. So why wasn't Alice? What was there to be angry about? Friends were *supposed* to help. She and Stevie were just being *friends*. Why couldn't Alice appreciate that?

She shook her head. This was the third day she'd been asking herself the same set of questions. Three days of absentmindedness was enough! There had to be an answer, and she hoped they'd find it today. Today was Tuesday. That meant they had riding class this afternoon. Alice was supposed to be there, but if what Stevie had heard was correct, Alice wouldn't be there. The one thing that bothered Lisa even more than the idea that Alice was angry with them was the idea that she might actually have meant it when she'd said she wasn't going to ride anymore. Horseback riding was the most important thing in the world to Lisa, and she couldn't bear the idea that somebody else might never do it again because of something she'd done—even if she hadn't meant to. That was the part that made Lisa feel the worst.

She had to talk to Stevie. She reached for the phone.

Stevie seemed to be in the same quandary that Lisa was.

"I can't believe she means she'll never ride again," Stevie said.

"But what if she did mean it? That means we caused it even if we don't know why."

"Then maybe we *ought* to know why," said Stevie.

"Maybe the 'why' is none of our business," Lisa suggested.

There was a long pause. One of Stevie's characteristics was her insatiable curiosity. It would never occur to her that there was something that wasn't her business.

But Lisa was beginning to see another side of what had happened. She and Stevie had just assumed that Alice's reasons for not jumping weren't important and

114

needed to be overcome. What if they were wrong about that? What if Alice had serious reasons for not wanting to jump and serious reasons for not wanting to talk about it? She quickly explained her thoughts to Stevie.

"But what kind of serious reasons could Alice have?" Stevie asked.

"None of our business," Lisa answered.

Stevie finally seemed to catch on. "You mean we were just meddling?" she asked.

"I guess that's the word," Lisa agreed.

Stevie was a girl of action. Once she'd reached a conclusion, she just had to act on it. "How soon can you get here?" she asked Lisa.

"Fifteen minutes," Lisa said. It would have been sooner since the two of them lived in the same neighborhood, but Lisa had to get dressed and pack her riding clothes for their afternoon class. She would be going to Pine Hollow from Stevie's house.

She changed and put her riding clothes in a backpack. She locked up the house and in fifteen minutes was at Stevie's door.

Stevie was waiting for her. "We have to talk to Alice," Stevie said, opening the door for Lisa. "We have to get her to come to class today. If she makes good on her threat and misses just one riding

115

class, it may take a lot longer to get her back into the saddle."

"We're going to have to apologize," Lisa said.

"A lot," Stevie agreed.

"We don't have any time to waste," said Lisa.

Together the two girls walked over to Alice's grandmother's house. They'd considered calling first, but they felt they had a better chance of succeeding in person.

Alice answered their knock.

"What are you doing here?" she demanded through the screen door.

"We came to say we're sorry," Lisa began.

"You should be," said Alice.

"We are," Stevie confirmed.

"We thought we were being helpful," Lisa said.

"You weren't," said Alice.

"We know," said Stevie. "We were just meddling."

"It isn't any of your business," said Alice.

"Yes," Stevie and Lisa agreed in a single voice. "We know that now," Lisa added.

"But if you don't ever ride again and we caused it, then it *is* our business," said Stevie. "You don't have to jump and you don't even have to talk to us. But we know that you love riding just as much as we do, and we can't stand the idea that you might not ride because of something we did that we shouldn't have done."

"Even though we *were* just trying to be helpful," Lisa finished.

"We're sorry," Stevie said again. "Really, we are."

Alice didn't say anything for a long time. She just stood there behind the screen door. Then, as they watched, Alice's eyes brimmed with tears.

Stevie was embarrassed, but understood that it would be wrong to say any more. They'd done their apologizing and said their piece. "Class starts at two," she said.

"Please come," Lisa added.

Alice stepped back and closed the door.

There was nothing for Stevie and Lisa to do then but to go to Pine Hollow, catch up on some chores, and hope that Alice would show up for class.

THROUGH THE HAZE Carole could feel a constant motion. The world around her swarmed. Bright lights above! She pushed herself toward them. She gasped for breath. Cool, fresh air entered her lungs.

She opened her eyes. It took a few seconds to understand. The constant motion came from the gurney beneath her. The bright lights were built into a ceiling. And the cool fresh air was from an oxygen mask that covered her nose and mouth. She was in a hospital. Sheila was on a gurney next to her, and her relatives were there, too, along with a mass of doctors and nurses.

"Hi, honey!" her father greeted her. "You're fine and so is Sheila, but you two gave us quite a scare."

"It was awful, Daddy," Carole said. "I kept going away and under."

"It was a riptide," Uncle Willie explained. "Those things'll pull out to sea before you know what's happening. And then, by the time you get out of its grasp, you're too exhausted to make it back to shore. You were very lucky."

Carole's memories of everything but the masses of powerful swirling water were vague. There had been a horse, though, she was sure of that.

Next to her, Sheila sat up and spoke to her.

"Hello!" she said.

Then Carole remembered. She and Sheila had somehow ridden the pony to shore. Sheila and her pony had braved the incredible force of tide and surf to save her.

"You guys rescued me, didn't you?" Carole asked.

"It was Maverick who did the rescuing," Sheila said. "I was just along for the ride."

"How is he?" Carole asked.

"The vet came to the beach to get him," Uncle Willie said. "Uncle Mitch and I followed the ambulance here. I told the vet we'd call later. Honestly, dear, I just don't know how he is. He collapsed on the

119

beach just like you two did. But he was alive. I never saw more determination in one animal in my whole life than I saw in that pony of yours."

"He loves me, Dad," Sheila said.

There were tears in Aunt Joanna's eyes. "I'll say," she agreed. "His love for you is strong enough to move mountains of water."

For Carole, the next couple of hours were spent at the mercy of an endless stream of well-meaning medical people. Carole was sure she was fine, but they insisted that she have every inch of herself checked. That meant X rays from head to toe and a careful examination of all of the scratches, abrasions, and contusions on her body. She was surprised to find how many places had been cut and scratched. Most of the cuts had probably come from being dragged along the sandy bottom of the ocean. None of them appeared to be serious, but they all got serious attention by the doctors and nurses.

Finally, she and Sheila were declared fit to leave.

"Sleep," the doctor said. "That's what they're both going to need a lot of."

Carole didn't doubt that for a minute. She was ready to start the prescription *almost* immediately. The "almost" meant that she wanted to put it off until she and Sheila had checked on Maverick.

Their parents couldn't object. After all, the pony had saved both girls' lives.

Uncle Willie drove them to the vet's clinic. They found the vet with Maverick, who was now lying down on the soft straw of a clean box stall. The vet was listening to him with his stethoscope. He took the instrument out of his ears and looked up at the visitors.

"How's he doing?" Sheila asked.

"Pretty well, considering," said the vet. "But he's tired. He took a lot of water into his lungs. The whole thing was a terrible strain on his heart. There is probably some lameness. Hard to imagine that he could endure such an exhausting trial without any effect on his mobility. I don't know what damage may have been done to any of his other systems, but my main concern is the exhaustion and his heart."

"Can I touch him?" Sheila asked.

The vet stood up and opened the stall door for Sheila. "Of course," he said, inviting her in.

Sheila went right to Maverick. She sat down by his head and began patting his cheek. He opened his eyes and looked up at her. He lifted his head ever so slightly. Sheila slid her legs under his face and then held his head on her lap. Maverick closed his eyes again and seemed to relax, reassured.

121

"You're going to be okay, boy," she said. "You are the strongest, bravest pony in the world. I never would have been able to save Carole without you, and she would be long out to sea without our help. You'll get better, Maverick. You just have to. If you could make it through the ocean, you can make it back to health. You just have to. I don't think I could—"

Sheila didn't finish the sentence, but Carole thought she knew what she was going to say. Carole had seen a lot of horses and owners and knew how close a relationship could form between horse and rider. She knew how much she loved Starlight. But she didn't think she'd ever seen anything like what she was witnessing right then. She'd seen Sheila and Maverick ride together as one. She'd seen the pony risk his life to do what Sheila asked him to do. And now she was seeing Maverick heal because Sheila asked him to. With every stroke of her hand, the pony seemed to find strength. It was awesome.

Carole was too tired to stand any longer. She just sat down on the floor of the stable and watched Sheila and Maverick. Her father, Aunt Joanna, Uncle Willie, and the vet watched in silence. It was a magical event, and only Sheila and Maverick mattered.

"Nobody's going to take you away from me," Sheila assured Maverick. "Never, as long as we live. We'll always be together. And if you are lame, I'll take care of you. I don't care if I never ride you again. I'll take care of you forever. I don't want another horse. I just want you." She was crying then. The tears spilled down her cheeks and landed on Maverick's soft brown coat, still crusted with salt from the ocean water.

Maverick snuggled closer to Sheila. Sick and tired as he was, he was nuzzling her, comforting *her*.

The vet crouched back down and put the stethoscope to Maverick's chest. He smiled.

"He's better," said the vet. "You're helping him, you know."

"He's helping me, too," said Sheila. Then she looked up at her parents. "You won't make me sell him now, will you? I've just got to keep him. You can understand that now, right?"

Aunt Joanna was crying. She couldn't answer. Uncle Willie answered for both of them.

"Any horse that's willing to risk his life just because you ask him to is a horse you can keep for as long as you want. Maverick has a home in our family. Guaranteed."

Sheila looked down at her horse. "Did you hear that, Maverick?" The pony took a deep breath and sighed. He closed his eyes.

"Is he okay?" Aunt Joanna asked the vet.

The vet reached out and put a hand on the horse's chest where his breathing was now regular, deep, and slow, just as it ought to be.

"He's okay. He's much better, in fact. And he's sleeping. That's what he needs most right now. Rest."

Very carefully, Sheila lifted his head from her lap and lowered it back onto the soft straw, patting him gently and talking calmly, aware that at some level he heard her voice and knew she was there and caring for him. She crouched next to the sleeping horse for a final farewell.

Carole listened. She was close, so she could hear what Sheila said as she patted her beloved pony while he slept.

> *Hush little baby, don't say a word.*
> *Mama's gonna buy you a mockingbird.*
> *If that mockingbird don't sing,*
> *Mama's gonna buy you a diamond ring—*

There was one more contented sigh from the pony. Then Sheila stood up. It was time to leave. It was time for Sheila and Carole to sleep, too.

JUST WHEN STEVIE and Lisa were going to stand by the door of Pine Hollow to see if Alice would show up, Mrs. Reg spotted them. Before the two girls could even say hello, Mrs. Reg began spouting a list of "little" jobs for them to complete before class. Since they felt they were still in hot water for their escapade on Sunday, they didn't dare argue. The next thing they knew, they were mixing feed grains in the grain shed. And then they were carrying a bale of hay to the feed room in the stable. And then they were mucking out Delilah's stall. By the time they finished these "little" jobs, they had to dash to tack up their horses for class.

The first they saw of Alice was in the schooling

ring. She was mounted and walking Comanche around to warm him up before class.

Both girls wanted to talk to her, to tell her how glad they were to see her, to say how right she'd been to decide to come back, and to apologize once again. None of these things got said, however, because Max entered the ring then and slapped his riding crop against his leg twice to signal the beginning of class. Max didn't allow any talking in his classes. Stevie and Lisa both felt that was a rule they shouldn't break just then. Class began.

Max started with the usual warm-up exercises. The riders walked, trotted, and cantered, and then switched among the gaits some until each rider was relaxed and comfortable with his or her horse and the horses were comfortable with their riders. Then he said that since this was a holiday week, he thought they ought to have some holiday spirit and would, therefore, be playing games for the rest of the class.

They began with follow the leader and, as usual, Stevie was picked to be the leader because Max knew he could count on her to do some fairly ridiculous things. She did not let him down. She took the eight riders in the class on a crooked trail around the ring and then right out of the ring by opening the gate. Three riders got eliminated right off the bat because they forgot to dismount at the gate as Stevie had. Stevie put down her reins and held her arms out like airplane wings, directing her horse with leg signals alone. Stevie was good at that and so was Topside. Most of the riders could handle it. A few could not. They were eliminated and ended up back in the ring, too.

It took another five minutes for Max to spot errors from the other riders, including the fact that Lisa was laughing. Alice, on the other hand, seemed to do everything just right. She and Stevie were the only ones left when Max declared the game ended, thanked Stevie, and congratulated Alice.

Then, since there were eight of them in class, Max formed two teams of four, and they began a series of relay races. In one of the races, the first rider had to ride to the far end of the course, pick up a water bucket from a stool, and carry it back to a teammate, who then had to ride it back and put it on the stool. The trickiest part of that one turned out to be putting the bucket back on the stool. Lisa approached the stool slowly and cautiously and managed the task the first time. Stevie was in such a hurry that she had to make Topside pass the stool four times before she could do it, and that included once when she had to dismount to pick the bucket up off the ground!

Then Max set up everybody's favorite game, and that was mounted squirt gun target practice. The problem was that all eight of the riders were issued squirt guns. While one member of each team rode forward to the targets and sent a stream of water as near as they could get to the bull's-eyes on the targets, the other three members spent their time squirting members of the opposite team. The opposing team returned "fire." The game ended in total chaos. The riders were all dripping wet, but laughing too hard to care. In fact, the driest part of the ring seemed to be the targets!

Lisa thought Max was trying to keep from laughing, but she couldn't be sure. It wasn't exactly like Max to laugh when all discipline got lost.

"Ahem," he said. That didn't do it. "Class!" he said, speaking louder and more forcefully. The riders continued squirting one another. "All right, you dirty rats!" he declared, bringing a super-soaker squirt gun out from behind his back and pointing it at the riders. There was silence.

Everybody was stunned to see their serious riding instructor standing there with a gigantic water gun in his hands.

"I just wanted to try this thing," Max said somewhat sheepishly. And with that, he turned and aimed

128

at the targets. A long and powerful stream of water emanated from the huge water rifle, found its mark, and annihilated one of the paper targets. The stream of water stopped. Max tipped the water gun so that the end of the barrel was near his face. Carefully, he blew away imaginary smoke, and then holstered the rifle.

"This here's mah town," he said, cowboy style. "What I say goes, understand?"

"Yes, sir!" the students replied, falling into character.

"An' ah say class dis-*missed!*"

Lisa looked at her watch. She always had fun in class, and it always seemed to go quickly, but she didn't think this class could have been more than fifteen minutes long. Her watch told her the truth. A full hour had passed by. She couldn't remember when she'd had so much fun in class before.

Reluctantly, the students walked their horses toward the stable. Lisa brought Barq up alongside Stevie and Topside.

"That was great, wasn't it?" Lisa asked.

"Totally fun," Stevie agreed.

"Carole's going to be so jealous that she missed it," said Lisa.

"Oh, don't feel sorry for Carole," Stevie said. "Remember, she's down in Florida, having a wonderful time and probably riding along the beach by the Atlantic Ocean without a care in the world!"

"I guess," Lisa agreed.

"Lisa? Stevie?" A voice called them from behind.

The girls turned around. It was Alice. They stopped and waited while she rode up to them.

Lisa and Stevie had both wanted to talk to Alice before class, but now that she was here and they all had had so much fun, they really didn't know what to say.

Lisa tried to speak for both of them. "I, uh—" she began.

"It's okay," Alice assured her. "I just wanted to thank you two."

"Thank us? What for?" asked Stevie.

"For making me come back," said Alice.

"You're welcome," Lisa said, and she meant it. It was nice to know that they'd done something right.

"BUTTER-PECAN ICE cream with blueberry-crumble cheesecake topping, marshmallow fluff, and Reese's Pieces," Stevie told the waitress at TD's.

"You want whipped cream and chopped nuts on that, too?" she asked.

Stevie grimaced, and shook her head. The waitress left the table with a proud grin on her face. This time she had succeeded in grossing out Stevie.

"Boy, it's nice to be home," said Carole.

"But didn't you have any fun in Florida?" Lisa asked.

"Yes, tell us all about it. Did you get to ride on the beach?" Stevie asked.

"Did I ever!" Carole began. She told them everything. She told them about the family party and the day at Disney World. Then she told them about her beach ride and her surfing and the riptide and her rescue by Sheila and Maverick.

"I never heard of a horse rescuing a swimmer!" Lisa said.

"Horses are good swimmers," Stevie said.

"This wasn't just swimming," said Carole. "This was heroism. In fact, the story got written up in the local newspaper. Somebody was taking pictures of us coming up out of the water. Aunt Joanna's phone was ringing this morning."

"With people wanting interviews and stuff?"

"No, people wanting to buy Maverick!"

"They wouldn't—" Lisa began.

"Not for a million dollars," Carole said. "Aunt Joanna is through with her meddling on that score." Then she told her friends about Midge and how nice she was and how Joanna kept meddling by trying to push Midge and her father together. "Dad and Midge were both nice about it because they didn't want to hurt Aunt Joanna's feelings, but Aunt Joanna just wasn't getting the hint. She's wonderful and all that, but she's the world's greatest meddler."

Lisa grimaced. "I think Stevie and I are competing

132

for that award, too," she said. Then she explained to Carole what had happened with Alice.

"We thought the jump around the curve was a perfect setup," Stevie said. "And it worked, too. Starlight loved it. Alice didn't."

"I know it was wrong," Lisa concluded. "But I'm still not sure why. I mean, when we three get together, it seems we do a lot of meddling. We're always fixing things that people didn't know needed fixing. Most of the time we seem to be right. Have we just been lucky until now?"

Carole shook her head. "It's not the same thing," she said. "Most of the time when we meddle, people know what it is that they want and we just help them get it. We do that with one another a lot. That's just part of what being in The Saddle Club means, right?"

Lisa and Stevie agreed with that.

"But this was different. See, Alice knew what she wanted, and we just refused to accept that."

Lisa thought it was generous of Carole to include herself in that with a "we." It was Carole's way of saying she would have made the same mistake.

"If we had just tried to talk her into changing her mind, that would have been one thing and that would have been okay. It was another thing altogether to try to trick her into changing her mind. No wonder she was angry."

The sundaes arrived then. The waitress had gone ahead and put whipped cream and chopped nuts on Stevie's. "I couldn't resist," she said. "But I didn't charge you for them."

"Thanks," said Stevie. "You're too good to me." Then, when the waitress left, Stevie leaned forward. "I knew she'd do that," she said. "That's how I can get extra toppings for free!" She giggled. Lisa and Carole thought she might actually mean it, too. Now they weren't so sure *who* had won.

Stevie took a bite. "Mmmmmm." Then she took a second. Lisa and Carole started their sundaes, too.

"Okay, so we did the wrong thing to Alice. But I still wonder why it is she doesn't want to jump," Stevie said after her third mouthful.

"I know the answer to that," Lisa said. Her friends looked at her and she told them. "It's none of our business."

"Very good!" Carole said. "See, we have learned something!"

"So what happened finally with Maverick?" Stevie asked. "Is Sheila going to keep on riding him?"

"Oh, this is the best part!" said Carole. "Maverick's going to be okay. The vet still thinks there's going to be some lameness for a while, but Maverick is definitely going to recover. He's also definitely going to be Sheila's pony for as long as he lives. But he's not going to be her only mount. Uncle Willie resolved the argument about Maverick. He's bought Sheila another horse—this time full-sized. Bright and early this morning, Sheila and I went to the stable that has horses for sale, and it didn't take long to find her the perfect horse. He's a seven-year-old gelding, a Thoroughbred mix. He's sixteen point two hands, a bay with a white mark on his forehead that looks a little like an upside-down comma—sort of like a wave. The vet checked him, and they bought him and moved him to Sheila's stable by the time Dad and I had to go to the airport this noon. It was something."

"What's she going to call him?" Stevie asked.

"I bet I know," said Lisa.

"What?" asked Carole.

"It's because of the marking, sort of," she began.

"Yes, it is, sort of," Carole agreed. "So what do you think it is?"

"Riptide," said Lisa.

"You're so smart. No wonder you're my friend!" Carole joked.

"Really?" Stevie asked.

"Really," Carole said. "The horse's name is Riptide.

And, believe me, that's the only riptide I ever want to ride again in my whole entire life!"

"Aw, come on," said Stevie. "You can't fool me. This whole thing was a setup, wasn't it?" She took another bite of her sundae and let her suggestion sink in.

"Setup? What do you mean?"

"I mean, you figured that the only way to solve Sheila's problem was to make her parents decide there was no way she could sell Maverick, so she'd just have to have a second horse. Then, when you got to the beach, the whole scheme came to you. You went out into the water, found the riptide, traveled a little out to sea, and let events take their natural course. Right?"

"You know what it was, Stevie?" Carole asked, playing along with the joke. "I just asked myself, 'What would *Stevie* do?' And it all came to me, just like you said. Then, in a matter of seconds, I risked my own life, to say nothing of Sheila's and Maverick's, just to have them go through a complicated and dangerous rescue so I could change my cousin's results at horse shows and make my aunt and uncle happy!"

"I knew it," Stevie declared. "See, when we Saddle Club members put our minds to it, there's just nothing we can't accomplish!"

ABOUT THE AUTHOR

BONNIE BRYANT is the author of more than fifty books for young readers, including novelizations of movie hits such as *Teenage Mutant Ninja Turtles* and *Honey, I Blew Up the Kid,* written under her married name, B. B. Hiller.

Ms. Bryant began writing The Saddle Club in 1986. Although she had done some riding before that, she intensified her studies then and found herself learning right along with her characters Stevie, Carole, and Lisa. She claims that they are all much better riders than she is.

Ms. Bryant was born and raised in New York City. She lives in Greenwich Village with her two sons.

THE
SADDLE CLUB

A blue-ribbon series by Bonnie Bryant

Stevie, Carole and Lisa are all very different, but they *love* horses! The three girls are best friends at Pine Hollow Stables, where they ride and care for all kinds of horses. Come to Pine Hollow and get ready for all the fun and adventure that comes with being 13!

- ☐ 15594-6 HORSE CRAZY #1 .... $3.25
- ☐ 15611-X HORSE SHY #2 .... $3.25
- ☐ 15626-8 HORSE SENSE #3 .... $3.25
- ☐ 15637-3 HORSE POWER #4 .... $3.25
- ☐ 15703-5 TRAIL MATES #5 .... $3.25
- ☐ 15728-0 DUDE RANCH #6 .... $3.25
- ☐ 15754-X HORSE PLAY #7 .... $3.25
- ☐ 15769-8 HORSE SHOW #8 .... $3.25
- ☐ 15780-9 HOOF BEAT #9 .... $3.25
- ☐ 15790-6 RIDING CAMP #10 .... $3.25
- ☐ 15805-8 HORSE WISE #11 .... $2.95
- ☐ 15821-X RODEO RIDER #12 .... $2.95
- ☐ 15832-5 STARLIGHT CHRISTMAS #13 .... $3.25
- ☐ 15847-3 SEA HORSE #14 .... $3.25
- ☐ 15862-7 TEAM PLAY #15 .... $2.95
- ☐ 15882-1 HORSE GAMES #16 .... $3.25
- ☐ 15937-2 HORSENAPPED! #17 .... $3.25
- ☐ 15928-3 PACK TRIP #18 .... $3.25
- ☐ 15938-0 STAR RIDER #19 .... $3.25
- ☐ 15907-0 SNOW RIDE #20 .... $3.25
- ☐ 15983-6 RACEHORSE #21 .... $3.25
- ☐ 15990-9 FOX HUNT #22 .... $3.25
- ☐ 48025-1 HORSE TROUBLE #23 .... $3.25

**Watch for other THE SADDLE CLUB books all year.
More great reading—and riding to come!**